S0-AES-600

ROWAN UNIVERSITY
CAMPBELL LIBRARY
201 MULLICA HILL RD.
GLASSBORO, NJ 08028-1701

Silent Close No. 6

Novels by Monika Maron available
from Readers International:

Flight of Ashes

The Defector

Monika Maron

Silent Close No. 6

translated by

David Newton Marinelli

readers international

The title of this book in German is *Stille Zeile Sechs*, first published in 1991 by S. Fischer Verlag GmbH.
© 1991 S. Fischer Verlag GmbH, Frankfurt am Main

First published in English by Readers International Inc., Columbia Louisiana and Readers International, London. Editorial inquiries to London office at 8 Strathray Gardens, London NW3 4NY England. US/Canadian inquiries to Subscriber Service Department, PO Box 959, Columbia LA 71418-0959 USA.

English translation © 1993 Readers International Inc.

All rights reserved

The editors wish to thank the Arts Council of Great Britain for their support.

Cover illustration: *The Red Model* by René Magritte. Reproduced by courtesy of the Boymans-van Beuningen Museum, Rotterdam.
Cover design by Jan Brychta.
Printed and bound in Malta by Interprint Ltd.

Library of Congress Catalog Card Number: 93-83085
British Library Cataloguing-in-Publication Data:
A catalog record for this book is available from the British Library.

ISBN 0-930523-93-8 Hardcover
ISBN 0-930523-94-6 Paperback

3 3001 00958 6511

for Jonas

Beerenbaum was buried in the part of Pankow Cemetery known as the memorial grove, an area reserved for the ashes of important persons like Beerenbaum. Although it was cold, I decided not to take the bus, and instead to walk the one or two miles between my apartment and Beerenbaum's future grave. I took the flowers I had bought out of the water - a small desiccated bouquet of freesia, I couldn't find anything else - dried the stems, and rolled them up in layers of newspaper to protect them from the cold. I like freesia; I don't know if Beerenbaum liked them. I decided to take a route that brought me within twenty yards of Beerenbaum's house, a slight detour, but the route I had taken twice a week for the last six months.

The house in which Beerenbaum lived was located in an exclusive residential section of Pankow popularly known as the "village," a name which sounds more affectionate than it was supposed to. Until the end of the 'fifties, the government lived in this semicircular area with several small streets and paths fanned out from it, behind fences and barriers protected by the army and police, until they moved outside the Berlin city limits. The only people left in this area immediately next to Niederschönhausen Palace were a few widows of former members of the government and once powerful men such as Beerenbaum. Some of the houses still had nameplates indicating their earlier, since deceased, inhabitants: the first President of the German Democratic Republic, the first Prime Minister, and the first Minister of Culture. Although it had been in good condition, the house of the first General Secretary was razed to its foundations following his death and a new, less attractive house built in its place. Of course this led to rumors. To be precise, they said so many bugs had been installed in the walls over the years that no one was able to remove them all, making the house unacceptable to new tenants. Most of the large houses in the "village" were refurbished as government guest houses. The smaller houses were inhabited by the caretakers whose job it was to maintain the large houses.

I began taking occasional walks in the "village" once it was opened to the public. The villa section was so quiet that no regulation was required to protect the permanent or changing tenants from traffic noise. But I wasn't attracted by the quiet alone. The old and new houses, the sterile, regular front-yard flower beds and bare flagpoles radiated an irritating unreality. The few pedestrians spoke quietly. The inhabitants were invisible; seldom did you see one drive out of a garage or return home; you never saw a child playing in one of the yards. Those living there were anonymous to outsiders; the only names to be found on the houses were bronze plates with the names of the dead. The only ones who occasionally tried to strike an acquaintance with strangers were a few plump, friendly cats. Relaxed or bored, they would sit on top of the boundary walls between the fences and let themselves be petted, or would hop down to follow passersby for a while. It was as bleak as a mining town after a gold rush. Except there were no doors or shutters to clatter in the wind. Order was maintained, as if by ghosts, as if those who had left were still here.

*

As I crossed Silent Close I noticed two cars parked in front of Beerenbaum's house - a large black vehicle with the chauffeur standing next to it smoking a cigarette and the crimson-red car belonging to Beerenbaum's son Michael. Michael had a pale, ascetic face with grey eyes that always made me feel uneasy, eyes that always looked directly at the person he was talking to, never aslant. Every time he trained his unmoving gaze on me, I thought he was blind or had artificial eyes. I had met him at Beerenbaum's perhaps four or five times, and about all I knew of him was that he was a senior army officer - his father called him Mischa - and that he had a taciturn son named Stefan, who looked much like him. I had never seen Michael Beerenbaum in uniform. If I had met him on the street, I would probably have taken him for a pathologist or a pastor, not a military man.

I continued walking, slowly, my head turned to the right, in the direction of Beerenbaum's house, which was no longer his house: No. 6. I felt nothing. I thought I felt relieved at Beerenbaum's death, that there was a simple, essential justice in him being dead and me alive, though I thought more than felt it. My hands were cold because I had forgotten my gloves, and the stems of the freesia were still moist. Perhaps he really didn't like freesia. He had bred roses. All old men with gardens breed roses. Why, I thought, why grow flowers, and why roses?

I first made the acquaintance of the rose-breeder Beerenbaum in the café where I used to sit outside on warm days, preferably during the late afternoon when the repatriates from the offices and factories went home by bus or streetcar. The café was close to a number of stops, and the many people returning home walked right past the café terrace. I had become so familiar with some of them over the years I could recognize them from afar by their gait or the kind of clothes they wore. Each spring I looked eagerly for changes in my secret acquaintances - women who had become pregnant, others who walked with their arm around a new man; families that had bought a dog over the winter. Some people I never saw again: they had moved or died; perhaps they were in prison.

I had also seen Beerenbaum several times without knowing who he was. I had noticed him because of his short gait - he walked from the knee, landing squarely on the soles of his feet. I have often observed this kind of walk in older men who, I assumed, had been sure of themselves during younger years and, as my mother would say, dashing - men who had been the boss of other people: head physicians or head cashiers or head engineers, head somethings, who were used to hearing themselves being addressed by title by their subordinates or families. Men who even in old age, when it is hard to walk, do not drag their feet along the pavement, but use the last bit of strength in their stiff bones to lift their feet a few inches above the ground, from their knees, before letting them fall again.

Walking with such a gait, which aroused my suppositions about his past, Beerenbaum slowly approached the café late last summer, newspaper under his arm, as I was drinking lemon tea and distractedly reading a book. He stopped in the entrance, looked around, came over to me - though there was an empty table in the right corner - and asked whether he might sit down. I had observed him other times trying to start conversations with strangers. Apparently he went to the café only to talk to strangers, and I had noticed that his interlocutors, most of whom were young, soon became listeners, following his animated words with the helpless smiles of those who have been out-witted.

I was anxious to find out how he would try to start a conversation with me, and in order to make that more difficult I read with ostenta-tious concentration, moving my eyes as if I were following the lines with them, occasionally turning a page without seeing more than a blur. Except for my eyes, all my senses were directed at the man sitting next to me, who kept his eyes firmly on mine so as to catch hold of them the instant they left the page.

He ordered apple pie with whipped cream; his newspaper lay on the table, unopened. The longer the silence between us continued, the more urgently I felt him asking me why I was refusing to talk, until I finally didn't know myself why I made things so difficult for this old man, though I was in fact curious about him. I did not find him likable: the corners of his mouth were sharp and downturned, bordering his lips like commas, and his bushy eyebrows had the same distant expression they had every time I had seen him.

The fact that I did not like the man was of little importance to me. I almost always found old men disagreeable, and of those few I have found agreeable I can remember every single one. My aversion was set off by certain optical and acoustical signals, for example the groping gait indicating former importance, a loud joviality with people in service jobs, such as saleswomen or waiters, who are thrown an embarrassing joke in a forced voice, as a dog is tossed a bone. Jokes about all the money his spendthrift wife has thrown away since they were married; the easy familiarity when saying "keep the change" while pushing a big bill across the table, eyes pointed in another direction. My aversion to these and similar symptoms of aging males turned to downright hostility as soon as I heard a certain grating, nagging tone, combining the insistent whining of a child with self-righteous irritability. I often felt uncontrollable hate. Even if I did not know the person and the tone of voice was not meant for me, I had to force myself not to ape him like a child. Once I did so in spite of myself, on a crowded streetcar. An old man was scolding his elderly wife for the bumpy ride: obviously, she was responsible. He whined incessantly to himself in a grating, strained voice, while the woman stood next to him, silent, furtively glancing left and right to gauge whether the other passengers were able to overhear him. The man repeated the same phrases over and over again, pausing just long enough that if the couple had been at home in the kitchen and not in this embarrassing situation, the woman might have had time to answer him. He seemed to know what the woman's answer would have been under those circumstances, so he reacted to her presumed responses, which made him even angrier.

I was standing behind him and could clearly feel the vibrations of his angry body in the air between us. First they penetrated my skin, then my flesh, until they reached my heart, which, suddenly enraged, brought my blood to a boil. It shot through my veins with such force that I could hear it seething behind my eardrums. Just as this anger had invaded me, so now it shot out of me in the man's own grating tones. "What did I tell you, what did I tell you?" I repeated his last phrase like a parrot, startled by my own strange voice, and, when the man and woman looked around at me in disbelief, I tried to cover my words with a rasping cough.

The waiter brought the apple pie and coffee. I lit a cigarette, which afforded the old man his first clear view of my eyes. As I had expected, he seized his chance.

He asked whether the book I was reading was interesting, and when I said it wasn't, he wanted to know why I was devoting so much attention to it. I said I didn't like this author, thus compensating my lack of aesthetic enjoyment with the assurance that the writer had failed again.

Without betraying by his expression whether he shared my judgment of the author, he began eating his apple pie with relish. I noticed that he used his left hand, while he held his right arm just under the table top with his other hand out of sight.

He asked whether my interest in literature was professional.

I said no.

Might he ask my profession?

He might, I said. I told him that my answer wouldn't be very enlightening. I no longer had a profession as such; I lived from clerical work and other services I could perform that did not require concentrated thought. He seemed to find that interesting. Or it aroused his suspicion. He watched me as he swallowed his apple pie. I expected him to ask me something else. He did not, so I began, without really wanting to, to explain further.

"Certain events in my life," I said, "have convinced me that it is a disgrace to think in return for money, and, in a higher sense, it is even prohibited."

*

Six months earlier I had in fact overnight come to a realization that rose the next morning as unmistakably as the sun in the sky of my banal existence, so much so that I asked myself where I could have been hiding it up to now - the realization that every day I took my one and only life to the Barabas research institute the way I threw kitchen garbage into the rubbish bin. That evening I had met one of the stray cats that lived in the garden quarter of our housing block, six or seven black speckled cats, whose black spots made their faces look like evil masks. One of them wore a spot around one eye, making it look like a highwayman. It was emaciated and timid with fur powdered yellow by the ashes in the rubbish bin where it looked for its food. One of them had black spots on both eyes, like a panda bear. She was the favorite on the block, spending most of her time at the kitchen window of the corner tavern, occasionally being thrown a piece of meat or fish by the cook. I came across the panda bear cat on my way home from the Barabas research institute. The bar was closed and, hungry, the cat followed me to my apartment. I sliced a pair of frankfurters into small pieces, poured milk into the bowl and put both in the kitchen. She ate quietly, drank the milk, caressed my feet several times as a thank you, and sat down in front of my door with her eyes fixed on the handle until I opened it for her.

The frankfurters were supposed to have been my dinner. The refrigerator was empty except for two lemons and a heel of liverwurst. The bread was moldy and the stores were closed. I found a bouillon cube and egg noodles and made soup. I thought - more out of casual habit than seriously - wouldn't it be great to be a cat. The sort of thing you think while making soup: to be a cat rather than lead this dog's life, to get your food anyplace, politely say thanks, then go back to your own patch and do what you want. I looked out the kitchen window. Six black-and-white cats were sitting in a circle on the lawn looking at each other. It seemed to mean something to them.

They weren't paid to sit there. When I sat in my 8-by-10-foot room in the Barabas research institute trying to convince myself I was interested in the second Saxon Communist Party Conference in 1919, I did so for money. I had to be interested in the party conference for the money I spent for the frankfurters I fed to cats so they could lie on the lawn at night doing nothing while I sat alone behind the kitchen window eating salty broth. The next morning, punctually at five after seven, I would leave my building to think for money in the Barabas research institute from seven forty-five a.m. to five p.m. under the supervision of Barabas and his slaves. As soon as I let myself be carried away by what had started out as nothing more than a casual, ill-tempered thought - wouldn't it be great to be a cat - I found the idea to be true, absurdly true and shocking. Every day I voluntarily closed myself up in a room about the size of a prison cell, which had been assigned to me like my subject, to which I had to devote eight hours of mental activity a day. "Colleague Polkowski, we have chosen you to research the development of proletarian movements in Saxony and Thuringia," Barabas had said the first time I sat across from him in his office fifteen years ago. That is what happened: I wasn't assigned a subject; it and the room were assigned to me. If I died, there would still be the subject and the room, just as they existed before me. They would be assigned to someone else who would be worn down by a narrow subject so as to ensure his physical existence, despite the fact that the only thing setting us apart from a cat is the gift of abstract thought. Our physical being is not unlike that of this furry creature.

If I was not lucky enough to be born with a silver spoon in my mouth, I at least wished to keep what sets me apart from cats. How did I, a person who was born free, manage to surrender my entire life to, of all people, Barabas, an ordinary greying family man who was promoted only because he combined contrariness with despotic pedantry. I switched back and forth between a western and a detective series on TV, devoting an equal amount of time to each. I kept thinking of the cat - especially when an animal appeared on the screen - and about the advantages her life had over mine. The cat came out ahead every time.

The night surrounded me like a sound-proof bunker. No one would talk to me until the next morning, and no one wished to be talked to. My room and subject were waiting for me in the darkness of the Barabas institute. Nothing about my life made sense to me anymore.

I did not get up the next morning. I stayed in bed, watched the sun rise over our street and penetrate the leaves of the trees in front of my window, to my pillow. I moved my head to the spot of sunlight and closed my eyes. I saw my blood in my eyelids - it was as red as cat's blood. Slowly, almost casually, I put together a sentence in my head: I shall no longer think in return for money. I spent the rest of the day in bed.

*

The old man stuffed a bite of apple pie into his mouth. I was surprised because I had always seen him talk and not listen. I was annoyed because I had lost my position of superiority so quickly, although I recognized how dangerous old men like this were for me. I gave them everything they wanted before they had time to ask me for it. This was one of the reasons

- perhaps the most important one - why I detested them. He leaned back and closed his eyes as if he were sunning himself. As I later found out, this was how he looked when he meditated. I reached for my book.

"Wait," he said, and turned toward me again. "I've talked to many young people, but no one has told me anything so strange as you have."

"I'm not young," I said.

"That may be," he said, "but compared to me you are."

That was true and, I thought, considering his age he could have been firmer in rejecting the modest estimate I had given of myself.

"So you don't think for money, but you do think. Before that you earned your money by thinking?" he asked, and although he tried to sound matter-of-fact, he couldn't hide the fact that he had suddenly begun to ask specific questions. I nodded, and before he could continue, I asked him how he earned his money. Or earns it, I added out of politeness.

"I've been earning it for forty years only through work," he said, underscoring the last two words by several firm taps of his forehead.

I was sure I could interpret a good deal from the man's facial expressions and gestures. I had long been suspicious of this man, though at first only because of his peculiar way of walking and his mania for buttonholing young people. His hands - I assumed that the right hand was similar to the left - reinforced my supposition: they were large, conspicuous hands that must have grasped stones and wielded an axe when they were still growing, yet which would no longer be capable of coarse work. I imagined a sharp contrast between their powerful shape and the withered skin covering them. Most of all, I was inspired by his face, an expression both familiar and suspicious, which could be interpreted as proud, self-confident, and strong-willed, on the one hand, and, on the other, arrogant and narrow-minded. Besides, there was a weariness between his eyes and chin more the result of age than disgust or defensiveness.

I had run into men with this facial expression throughout my life. My father's last face was like this. I was almost certain of it. Moreover, I was driven to annoy the old man with what I knew about him in order to challenge the dominant position in our conversation which I had relinquished to him owing to my inherent weakness in dealing with old men. "May I take a guess at your biography?" I asked. He looked surprised.

"Go right ahead, if you think you can."

"Poor background," I said, "perhaps the son of a worker; mother was a housewife. Finished primary school. Trained as a lathe operator or mason, perhaps as a carpenter. Joined the Communist Party when you were eighteen or nineteen. Emigrated or sent to a concentration camp after Hitler came to power in 1933." No, not to a concentration camp, I thought, his face doesn't have the permanent disgust I have seen on the faces of other survivors. "Probably emigrated," I said. He didn't look like someone who had made his way in France or America; they looked different. Either one looked different before that or because of the time abroad. I placed the man at my table in Moscow, perhaps in the notorious Hotel Lux, where Communists from around the world were lodged and which became a death trap for many. "You emigrated to the Soviet Union," I said, "and lived for a time in the Hotel Lux. Returned to Germany in 1945. You were then assigned to important posts wherever the Party needed you."

He smiled when I mentioned the Hotel Lux, as if he had caught me cheating. "You know who I am," he said, either out of vanity or disappointment.

I protested I knew nothing more about him than what his appearance had told me, but as he did not believe I was that perceptive, I did not dispel all his doubts. Incidentally, I was wrong about one thing, he said. He was not eighteen or nineteen when he became a Communist, he was seventeen.

Irritated, he reached for his fork to finish the last crumbs of apple pie on his plate. Either he thought I was making a fool of him, or he was uneasy because he couldn't explain my modest knowledge of his life. Although I now incontestably held the advantage, I was unable to set the rules. He was annoyed. I therefore had to offer him a compromise if I wished to learn why the man assumed people knew his identity. I decided to ask a direct question, smiling and in a cheerful tone of voice. Being a well-known personality, would he be so kind as to tell me his identity, I asked, because I am a terribly amateurish magician unable to guess real secrets.

He put down his fork, leaned back and said with a triumphal gleam in his eye: "My name is Beerenbaum, Herbert Beerenbaum."

"Professor Herbert Beerenbaum?" I asked.

Instead of an answer, he gave me his calling card. He said he was looking for someone to do secretarial work two days a week, no thinking involved, and he was willing to pay five hundred marks a month. He would be happy if I would accept his offer. He had a contract to write his memoirs and I could see for myself... He drew his trembling right hand into sight. He then placed the money for the apple pie, whipped cream, and coffee on the table and left. I never found out what moved him to make me this offer. Was it my statement that I no longer wished to think in return for money, or my mysterious knowledge of some particulars of his biography?

My precarious financial situation would not have been reason enough to offer my services to replace Beerenbaum's trembling right hand, to serve this Professor Beerenbaum who until three years ago had been a powerful man at the side of other powerful men, someone who was reputed to have been a brilliant rhetorician and inflexible Stalinist during his time - and it truly was his time. And this despite the fact that I surmised time and age had moderated his views, that like his throat his rhetoric had dried up and his intransigence turned brittle once his spine had begun to harden, the same way his power had slowly vanished with the death of his generation. Nonetheless he was still the man Beerenbaum, and I asked myself what had moved him to give this work to me of all people. Of course, he would have no problem having someone assigned to him from an institute for secretarial work, without having to pay her. Why was I wanted, who had turned my back on being useful and rejected goals once and for all, to write down his memoirs in my own hand?

Perhaps he was contentious and able to articulate his thoughts only by contradicting other people, and he hoped I would be a mirror for his shadowboxing, the way a torero wields a red cape, shuffling in front of him to arouse the bull in him into a fighting mood. Once he noticed I neither wanted to reflect or shuffle, he would invest his five hundred marks more profitably by replacing me with a secretary financed by the state. Or the man had been chastened and wished to make amends for something. But not even a devout Christian who believed that good deeds will be rewarded, much less an atheist like Beerenbaum, would assume that he could make amends by hiring an absolute nobody for five hundred marks a month.

*

Beerenbaum's burial was scheduled for two. I walked briskly because of the cold, arriving at the cemetery entrance fifteen minutes early. Crowds of old people walked along the

cemetery road to the chapel, carrying bouquets
made of artificial flowers or wreaths. A tired,
decrepit protest march in Beerenbaum's honor.
I preferred to spend the remaining time outside
the cemetery to spare myself the painful gloom
exuded by waiting mourners. A doleful road
where there was nothing to be seen except the
cemetery walls that continued until the road
turned right to Schönholz and where, suddenly,
a piece of the other, the only, the real Wall
stood, only to disappear a few hundred feet
further on behind housefronts. It took me a
long time to decide whether or not to go to
Beerenbaum's burial, whether my presence
would not be considered inappropriate, even a
provocation, and why I should risk arousing
such suspicions.

A year ago I had not known the man, I had
known only his name, like other names that
appear frequently in the newspapers. Then he
infested my life like the plague. I needed this
leave-taking. I had even visited him in the
hospital, because I hoped the terrifying tension
between him and myself could be relieved at
the very last minute, extinguished as a mistake.
Beerenbaum had lived in an exclusive area, he
was buried in a separate section of the cemetery and, of course, he was also treated in a
special hospital closed to the general public

that didn't even smell like an ordinary hospital. There was a net around his bed. The shriveled Beerenbaum lay inside it as in a crib; the human being recognizable as the worn-out material it is made of: the gelatine of the eyes, with the sockets showing, the skin like parchment, separated from the flesh, the network of blue veins underneath the transparent temples, the skull pushing against the flabby skin, and already visible like the face of death beneath the one that had belonged to Beerenbaum during his life. They had removed his dentures, probably to keep him from choking on them in case he fainted. He attempted to smile with his bared puckered lips when I placed my flowers on his night table. He was barely alive. It was impossible to hate him.

I wanted to sit on the chair next to his bed, but he knocked on the side of the bed with his palm and made some gurgling sound that could have meant "Come here." I thought that he also wished to be reconciled before taking leave of me, and I felt relief. I sat down on the corner of the bed, carefully, fearing that the slightest jarring movement would cause this sore body pain. I said I was terribly sorry, I also said I'd made life very difficult for him during the months we'd known each other. I couldn't sleep nights because I was afraid I was one of the causes of his heart attack. That was a lie. I hadn't lost a minute's sleep over him. At this moment I was ashamed. I would have taken everything back I had accused him of in my sadistic zeal - the slaughter in the Hotel Lux, the power-hungry children of the proletariat who had worked their way to the top, their fear of everything they didn't understand, which is why they banned so much. Now that he was dying, I would have taken back every sentence to be reconciled with him for my farewell. If Beerenbaum's hand hadn't suddenly lunged for me like a greedy, white-skinned beast.

A soldier was looking in my direction through binoculars from the window of the watchtower behind the Wall. I felt I was being observed, so I turned around. In the meantime, twenty or thirty cars had parked in front of the cemetery, including a number of black limousines and Michael Beerenbaum's crimson-red car. I forbade myself to think about Beerenbaum's hand. I was here because I needed this farewell, because I needed to know that he was really buried and out of this world. I had to know whether someone was weeping for him and who that someone was.

*

I planned to do a lot during the summer and ended up accomplishing nothing. The piano stood in the corner, elegant and useless. Every day I sat down in front of it, opened the lid, played the "Flea Waltz," with both hands, though only the first third, and closed the lid. This was the piano the Count had bought for his bride Tsugiko. It had been exposed to dampness and fluctuations of temperature wrapped in blankets in a coal cellar for five years. Then the Count left the instrument to me after he had heard nothing from Kyoto for two years, meaning that he had stopped hoping Tsugiko would come to Berlin and they would be married. But if Tsugiko did show up one day, the Count's voice broke, well, I'd know, in this case and only in this case would he have to ask me to give it back.

One of my biggest unfulfilled wishes as a child was to own a piano, but, most of all, to be able to play one. Having left the Barabas institute once and for all, I now had all my time to myself and I decided to learn to play the piano to the extent my years and meager (or so I feared) talent allowed me. Two storeys above me lived Thekla Fleischer, a certified piano teacher, a woman of undefined years and an equally undefined figure because she always

arrayed her body in broad garments which had
been elegant in days gone by. During the ten
years I had known her, her face still looked like
that of a young nun, though the glasses she
wore in front of her ever moist eyes had gotten
thicker over the years. This summer, though,
Thekla Fleischer underwent a miraculous transformation. She would warble "It's a beautiful
day today" to me when I met her on the front
lawn of our building, even in the pouring rain,
as she scurried past me, as if tweeting a bird's
song at dawn. Suddenly, Thekla Fleischer started wearing tight-fitting skirts, even jeans, as if
someone had told her the best thing about her
was her wide hips. As long as I had known her,
she had worn her smooth hair in a simple knot.
Now she had a permanent wave that made her
grey hair stand up on her head like a dandelion.
Thekla Fleischer did all the foolish things
people do when they fall in love. Although I
couldn't imagine what kind of man had been
attracted to the charms of Thekla Fleischer's
protracted virginity, the only explanation for
her ludicrous, touching transformation was that
someone had entered her life. I thought it
would be tactless to spoil her joy by having her
teach me the rudiments of playing the piano.
My request would have been possible if I had
wanted only to polish my playing and reinforce

her feelings by performing Beethoven's *Für Elise* or Liszt's *Liebestraum*. But "Twinkle, twinkle little star" or "Bah, bah, black sheep" would be excruciating for Thekla Fleischer's love, perhaps the only one in her life.

I also wanted to tackle the recitatives to *Don Giovanni* this summer. I had heard on the radio that *Don Giovanni* was sung only in Italian for lack of a good German translation. The biggest problem was the recitatives, considered untranslatable within the given rhythms. This got me thinking about how to solve the problem. I didn't know Italian, I didn't like opera, and the only thing I knew about recitatives was the part of an opera given this term. I assumed that everyone who had been unsuccessful in translating the recitatives to *Don Giovanni* knew Italian, was an expert on Mozart's operas, and knew everything about recitatives and their being untranslatable. I therefore considered my ignorance of all of the above as a fortuitous prerequisite to succeeding in this impossible task through unconventional means. I hoped that my talent in pinning down and imitating the peculiarities of other people's speech melodies would help me. If I were able to grasp the Italian recitatives as a unity in their fusion of speech and music, ignoring both rules and models, I should be able to find a German version. If, like my predecessors, I were to fail, I would still be initiated as few other connoisseurs into the secret of the untranslatability of the recitatives to *Don Giovanni*. I found both success and failure equally enticing, especially as my interest was purely that of a novice, unspoiled by professional ambition or financial need.

I began to look for materials for my project during the spring, including a complete recording of the opera, a bilingual libretto, a score, and an Italian-German dictionary. By the end of the summer I still had not found the score, the dictionary, or the Italian libretto - I had bought a German version in a used book shop. I could have asked Bruno: he knew everything there was to know about Mozart; he even knew lesser-known works, including their Koechel numbers, after only a few bars over the radio. Bruno couldn't listen to *Don Giovanni* sung in German without comparing - after, or, better still, during the performance - the librettos. Bruno had attended several performances of Felsenstein's production of *Don Giovanni* in German a few years ago, which led me to believe that he might have all the materials I needed for my project.

Still I didn't ask Bruno. I didn't wish to let him spoil my fun, and Bruno would have spoiled it, I was sure of that. Although he understood Italian, knew *Don Giovanni* by heart, although he could read scores and played the piano since he was a child, he would never have dared to touch the *Don Giovanni* recitatives. He despised dilettantes, in fact he considered them dangerous. Fearing that he too was a dilettante, Bruno restricted himself to passive enjoyment. He was even loathe to write letters, because in Bruno's mind every written word that went beyond telegrams and filling out questionnaires was literature. Loathe to submit to this standard, he refrained from writing. Similarly, Bruno did not sing, he never danced, and I never found doodles on his note pads of the kind most people scribble during boring meetings or phone calls.

When I told Bruno about my plan to learn the piano, he tilted his head to his right shoulder and looked at me for a while, as though he could make me out better with his eyes one on top of the other. He returned his head to its normal position and sighed: "Ah, Rosa, you're another one of these people who only understands what they do themselves. Why not listen to Rubinstein or Glenn Gould play piano concertos instead of banging on the instrument yourself? There's this mania everywhere you look to possess things. You own only those things you can touch with your own hands. Grabbing instead of grasping. Too bad, Rosa."

I could imagine Bruno's comments on my tackling the recitatives to *Don Giovanni*, so I preferred instead to wait for the fortuitous chances I would need to start my work.

With my plans for piano lessons and the recitatives to *Don Giovanni* coming to nought, I should have been able to concentrate on my third project. The bright red complete edition of the works of Ernst Toller stood out on my bookshelf. But I never felt strong enough to ask myself the question I had read many years ago in Toller, which had crept into the convolutions of my brain as stealthily as a cockroach, where, much as I tried to exterminate it, it has been multiplying ever since.

Must the agent suffer constant guilt? Or, in order to avoid guilt, perish?

I had come across Ernst Toller when I had to write a paper on the Munich Soviet Republic for the Barabas institute. I was fascinated less by his works of fiction than by his calamitous fate, one he seemed to have been born to, which pursued him ineluctably until his death in the Mayflower Hotel in New York, where he hanged himself with his bathrobe tie. I don't know why I expected this biography to shed light on my own life, but that's how it was. Bruno said my predilection for Toller was an expression of my longing to act.

"In that case I could just as easily be interested in Robin Hood," I said.

"He would be no consolation for you," Bruno said. "Toller consoles because he failed."

This had been on my mind ever since I finally left the Barabas institute. I felt healed and ill at the same time, like a person who has had a slowly growing tumor removed from his brain, yet suffers afterwards from the emptiness. Without the operation he would have died; yet the symptoms he feels after the operation - dizziness, impaired coordination, disorientation - result from the cure, so that when he feels especially bad he begins to doubt whether the operation was really necessary.

I thought Bruno might be right in suspecting that all I sought in Toller's life was consolation against the inactivity to which I had condemned myself, yet I was annoyed at the indulgent tone in which he described my longing to act, as if this were a third eye or a club foot or some other congenital defect.

Ernst Toller's collected works remained untouched on my bookshelf. I spent almost the entire summer in the country, where Bruno and I had bought a house six years ago in a virtually deserted village near the Polish border. We had kept it after we were separated.

*

I had been back in the city only a few days when I met Beerenbaum in the café. Upon my arrival home I ran into Thekla Fleischer in front of our building getting into a taxi with a silly grin on her face. The taxi driver, who seemed to know how to react to Thekla Fleischer's state of mind, drove off with a screech, shooting out of the narrow street. I imagined Thekla Fleischer sitting in the cab, her heart beating and with all the other attributes of someone who is excited, approaching the object of her love at thirty-five or forty miles an hour. I imagined her carefully removing her glasses from her nose, which were steamed up in her excitement, and cleaning them with a purple embroidered handkerchief. She was smiling and you could tell how hard she was trying not to tell the cab driver how happy she was. Then she rummaged through her handbag until she found a tiny bottle from which she once again - it must have been the third or fourth time, the bottle was almost empty - dabbed herself behind her ear lobes with the fragrant fluid. Hands trembling, she closed it again and nonchalantly dropped it into her handbag.

I wished Thekla Fleischer the best of luck with the person for whose sake she was making a fool of herself, even though it stood in the way of my finally learning the piano.

*

The woman wearing the apron dress with linden-green butterfly sleeves, who had opened the door for me and called to the Herr Professor with a voice that sounded like a rattling bucket, poured coffee for Beerenbaum, stirred two lumps of sugar in the cup, and placed a piece of apple pie on Beerenbaum's plate. She then left the room without a word.

"Please, help yourself," Beerenbaum said.

Beerenbaum's living room resembled that of my parents. The dark veneered wall unit with glass doors containing sparkling dinnerware, the sofa set covered in synthetic satin, the rag wool tablecloths on the square table, the dark red Persian carpet, the heavy curtains with the stylized floral pattern - these were all familiar to me. The pattern of the Bulgarian tapestry was the same as my parents', only bigger. And the colorful, lacquered Russian doll contained nine other dolls which stood next to each other in a straight row on the wall unit shelf. The Babushka my father had received when he had had to go to Leningrad with a delegation of teachers shortly before his death held only four.

But instead of a reproduction of van Gogh's *Sunflowers*, like the one that had hung over the sofa in my parents' living room for twenty years, there was a post-Impressionist landscape depicting a rusty-looking autumnal beech forest beneath a cloudless blue sky.

"I have left everything the way it was when my wife died," Beerenbaum said.

Because I thought I had to, I asked when his wife had died.

"Three years ago," he said. He had just had a stroke himself so he wasn't even able to bury her, after they had belonged to each other for more than fifty years.

He actually said it: "belonged to each other." I thought those might have been the words his wife had used. He wore a wine-red cardigan that revealed his curved back and dangling shoulders like the bones beneath the fur of an old animal; for the first time I saw how frail he was. It occurred to me that my father had worn a similar cardigan and similar slippers - Bordeaux-red leather slippers. I thought that I had been sitting like this before, that I ought to know how the conversation continued, because I had had the same one before, but I didn't know, I really didn't know what I was supposed to say.

His trembling right hand resting on his thigh was like a third person in the room. I tried not to pay attention to the piece of flesh that seemed shaken by a constant aversion; I stirred milk into my coffee for a long time and waited, determined not to talk about anything I wasn't asked about. He said the usual sort of thing - he was certain we would get along with each other; he only wanted my dexterity with a pen. Of course, this went without saying, if I wished to make critical remarks, speak up, he would be grateful for any comments, after all, he wasn't a writer, and it was only his duty to bear witness for future generations that made him resort to the pen, ha ha, a symbolic pen, of course, I'd know what he meant.

So he did want my mind, after all. My thought was less ghoulish than the sentence containing it. All the same, he wanted my mind, one way or the other, and I acted as if I hadn't heard that.

After finishing our coffee we went into his study, a square room condemned to eternal darkness by a stout copper beech in front of its single window. He sat down at the desk in front of the window. The sparse light from outside and the early twilight reduced Beerenbaum to his contours, like a cardboard figure in a shooting range. He motioned to me to sit down at a small round table dominated by a type-writer, a gigantic fossil of a Rheinmetall literally redolent with history.

He began as I had expected he would. Beerenbaum came from the Ruhr; his father was a miner, his grandfather was a miner, his mother a devout Catholic, his grandmother also. Beerenbaum was born in 1907 to a poor family. Every proletarian family was poor at the time, including mine. I wasn't terribly interested in what Beerenbaum dictated, which I had to write down by hand to be able to read it back to him for corrections. Although I could not see his face, I was certain Beerenbaum was observing me. I tried to hide my lack of interest without having to pretend I was interested.

Now and again, Beerenbaum would ask me whether I preferred this or that word. My answers were always noncommittal. Either I didn't know or both were possible. He accepted that.

From then on I worked for Beerenbaum two afternoons a week, Tuesday and Friday. I would ring his doorbell at three on the dot. On Tuesdays the housekeeper opened, while Beerenbaum came to the door on Fridays because the housekeeper went home early that day.

Our work, to the extent I can use the term to describe what we did together, was almost harmonious. If I ignore the fact that I felt constantly watched by Beerenbaum, he kept strictly to our agreement. I was to write and that was all. Each afternoon he dictated five pages, which led me to conclude that he prepared himself during the other days of the week for our meetings with the discipline of a man who is used to considering his work important. I was glad, after the fact, that I had accepted Beerenbaum's offer. Although I did not talk to anyone about it, I had a hard time getting used to my new life, in which I was completely free to dispose of my own time. I still got up every morning at six-thirty, and the evenings I stayed up very late I seldom managed to get back to sleep. Everything in my life had started at eight in the morning: kindergarten, school, even university, as well as my working hours at the Barabas institute. All the same, ten or fifteen years ago I could sleep until noon at weekends or when on vacation. But at some later point this habit had become a law which as soon as I broke it invariably brought punishment in the form of nightmares. Just beneath the surface of sleep I was driven through them like someone drowning. And scarcely had my smarting brain fought its way through the confusion in the saving knowledge that I really didn't have to fear what I had just dreamed, the next nightmare followed like a wave that closed both nose and mouth, preventing me from breathing. I allowed this to happen until, after an indeterminable period, beaten and exhausted, I finally emerged into daylight.

The weight of dreams became greater the less I could remember them. Even if I succeeded in dragging the last ones into consciousness, all that was left of their predecessors was a diffuse depression that often accompanied me the whole day like my shadow; I therefore preferred to get up at six-thirty, or seven at the latest, in order to bear the entire day. Sometimes I would sit at the breakfast table until noon thinking about something meaningful to do. It went without saying that I had to learn languages and read all of world literature. But, most of all, I wanted to act, though I didn't know what to do. This longing to do something existed, insatiably, against my will. I considered it absurd, especially since there was something of a redeeming power about it, as if, after the fact, a single act could lend meaning to what had consisted of an amorphous infinity of coincidences, which now lay behind me like the greater part of my life. My first thought of acting was always linked to the image I had of a rearing white horse spurred on by its rider to jump over an abyss. The picture came from a book of fairy tales I had been given - I think by my Aunt Ida - when I started school.

I was now occupied two afternoons a week without having to think about what to do. I was also comforted by the thought that I now had a regular, if modest, income.

*

The sound of my rapid steps on the hard sand path echoed through the silent cemetery. The people in front of the chapel had begun to move. Almost motionless until now, the small groups, distributed over an area of from sixty to a hundred feet, slowly began to condense into a large black mass. This in turn became a many-linked chain structured according to rank and proximity to the deceased, which re-appeared, as if pulled by an invisible hand, only to vanish, link by link, into the wide-open chapel portal. I walked faster, unwrapping the freesia from layers of newspaper as I went, not knowing what to do with the newspaper. I crumpled the paper as best I could and stuck it in my coat pocket. The man whose job it was to lock the chapel door kept it half open for me, with a look of urgency on his face, forcing me to unseemly haste. All the chairs were taken. I had to stand. The only other person standing was the doorkeeper, who probably was not permitted to sit under any circumstances, meaning that there was one chair too few - mine. I thought it was perhaps a mistake to have come, that I did not belong to those who had the right to bid a final farewell to Beerenbaum, because rather than mourning his death, I welcomed it.

The chapel was heated. There was a small iron furnace in the corner to the right of the entrance, with a red-hot pipe running halfway up the wall outside. The musicians, a string quartet and an organist, had taken their places near the furnace. All five wore cheap-looking tuxedos stretched tightly over their stomachs. They looked at their music, the doorkeeper, and me with a gravity you could tell had been paid for. Their looks seemed to indicate they considered me to be one of them, because they knew that I was more a clown or entertainer than a mourner. Beerenbaum's portrait hung on the wall opposite the entrance, a smiling Beerenbaum wearing a dove-grey suit. The photographer had changed his hair from white to silver. The picture radiated a light, a conciliatory brightness, intensified by the crepe band hung obliquely across the frame. The coffin, surrounded by red carnations and white calla, lay on a pedestal below the picture. Everything looked cheap, including the coffin decoration, with its unimaginative symbolism of death and class struggle, although the flowers were in fact genuine. I imagined how Beerenbaum looked lying under the lid of the coffin between silk cushions. I didn't know if they still dressed the dead in a shroud or whether Beerenbaum had been dressed in one of his suits, perhaps the dove-grey suit in the picture. Beerenbaum lay in his dove-grey suit between silk cushions in a closed coffin and had ceased to be Beerenbaum. As, in my eyes, Ida had stopped being Ida. Her hand in my hand was the same, and yet, from one second to the next, it was no longer Ida's hand. It had left Ida, had vanished, without a trace or shape, and had left what remained of Ida behind. I had to have what remained of Ida transformed into ashes, because that was her wish. Cremation is progressive, she said. I always presumed this wish was less the result of her faith in progress than her fear of worms. If I had been able to remember the burial of my paternal grandmother, as Ida and my mother did, I certainly would have been less affected by the absurd fear of suffering on the crematorium grill.

My grandmother died a few weeks after the end of the war, in June or July. The summer of '45 was really hot, my mother said. My grandparents lived in a village near Berlin. My grandmother was buried there too. My mother said that the coffin was kept in the cemetery chapel, probably the coolest place there was, during the two or three days between her death and burial. Before the funeral my grandfather kept running around the coffin with a dustpan and brush, bending down again and again to sweep something away, silently, with no visible reaction. Ida and my mother thought it was nothing. They thought that the war and the death of his wife had muddled the old man's brain. It wasn't until the sermon, when they noticed that the pastor kept an unseemly distance from the coffin and that he avoided looking in the direction of the deceased and her next of kin, that they began to suspect what soon became terrible certainty - fat, round, white worms were constantly dropping from the coffin. My mother told me she never understood how the worms could have gotten so big in the few days the woman had been dead.

The string quartet got ready to play; and the organist casually placed his fingers on the harmonium keyboard. The first violinist gave the cue to play "Immortal Sacrifice." Beerenbaum, an immortal sacrifice. Whose sacrifice? Between the silk cushions under the coffin lid lay the mortal remains of an immortal dressed in a dove-grey suit. The shoulders and backs of those seated in front of me showed they were moved; here and there a hand raised a handkerchief to a face. Those who wept were weeping for their own deaths. Half of Beerenbaum's mourners would receive a similar burial. Everyone here would go to the grave as aged sacrifices, kept alive at all costs in special hospitals far beyond statistical life expectancy. I was surprised death managed to keep up with our absurd way of dealing with it.

I was glad to be standing behind these people rather than sitting among them. Although I couldn't see their faces, I could feel every slight movement of their bodies and heads. Moreover, I would have felt awful if someone else had been the last to enter the chapel and had to stand. No one belonged here less than myself. Still, I thought, still I have the right to be here. I wasn't simply saying farewell to Beerenbaum; I was putting him out of my life where he had taken a place long before we had met, a place he had taken as if it had been his own.

*

Beerenbaum sat - all I could see was his shadow - behind his desk dictating. For weeks he had been reveling in his childhood while I was trying to figure out why he thought it was worth retelling. He eulogized his family's poverty as though he wished to apologize for his later prosperity, just as I felt every detail he told about his early life existed only as a function of his coming fate - his early interest in politics, his thirst for knowledge, the teacher who recognized his gifts, his sense of justice and, of course his class instinct, that a worker's son in the Ruhr, to use Beerenbaum's words, was born with.

"Class instinct," what a horrible expression, the deadly weapon my father used to use when he attempted to support his assertion that Kafka's books, of which he probably never read a line, were decadent, harmful literature, if indeed literature at all. His class instinct told him so. His class instinct also told him jazz was a type of music unsuited to the socialist awareness of life because it was slave music. Also that my boyfriend Josef, a tall, thin boy with large feet and intelligent eyes that sometimes shone defensively (my father considered this arrogance) wasn't right for me. My father used the word instinct to mean infallibility. You don't need a reason when you are infallible, nor can it be refuted.

I was my own biggest obstacle to my resolve to serve Beerenbaum's memoirs only with my hands. While Beerenbaum was not bothered by my refusal to use my intellect, soon ceasing to involve me in choosing this or that word, I found it progressively harder not to contradict him. I suffered so much at the silence I had imposed upon myself that I was unable to suppress an occasional gentle groan, which encouraged Beerenbaum to ask whether I objected to what he had said. I said I had back pains or pretended to get angry at a spelling mistake. Beerenbaum accepted these explanations, yet each time I lost control he continued dictating sentences even more revolting than the one that had made me groan. Once he said, "Even as a little lad I knew that my heart was on the left and the enemy on the right." As I wrote this down, my diaphragm began to flutter nervously. At first, because I would like to have laughed, but then, because I refused to laugh, my diaphragm constricted regularly until I had violent hiccups. Beerenbaum had Mrs Karl, the housekeeper, bring me a glass of sugared water that made me feel sick once my hiccups finally stopped. Of course, my reaction was exaggerated. In 1914, when Beerenbaum was a little boy, one's heart was on the left and the enemy was on the right. If Beerenbaum had been any old man and not Professor Beerenbaum, I probably would have tolerated the bathos of this sentence. But when Beerenbaum, his lips sweetly pursed, called himself a little lad, I felt sick. I couldn't imagine Beerenbaum as a little boy. Beerenbaum's boy's body was still topped by an old head with heavy eye pouches and a tired, self-righteous expression on his mouth. So long as Beerenbaum talked about his childhood, I was seldom aroused by the facts he spoke about, which were either commonly known or private and innocuous. Almost always it was the tone, the self-assurance of his choice of words, the sentimentality and simple-minded metaphors that made me lose control of my diaphragm.

I had grown up with this kind of language. My parents spoke it as soon as they turned to such grandiose topics as running the household or rearing children. There was no distinct boundary between private speech and this other language. For example, my mother would tell my father that her young colleague B. had a new boyfriend, adding, as she returned a plate to the cupboard: "Really a good comrade," which sounded as if she had meant to say: Really a good boy.

Or my father would come home and complain about the dirt in the metro stations - "our people" simply wouldn't understand that the struggle for Communism begins with candy wrappers.

My parents used their unnatural language with me when I needed educating. My father could speak to me only for pedagogical reasons - he had nothing else to tell me - so that I still associated this high-sounding gibberish with him at a time when I was too old to be educated and when he confined his verbal contact with me to saying hello and good-bye. He also congratulated me annually on my birthday and wished me a happy new year. Since then we no longer argued; my mother said she was happy we finally understood each other better.

I suspected Beerenbaum was intentionally provoking me to force me to contradict him one day so I would at last serve him with both my head and my hands for his five hundred marks. Keeping the seating arrangement as it was - me at the small round table, him at his desk in front of the only window - which concealed him from me in his shadow, I was unable either to confirm or deny my suspicions

about possible changes of expression on his
face. I thought I occasionally heard a forced
gaiety in his voice, but I wasn't sure. Rarely
when he laid his head back or on one shoulder,
did a beam of light glide over his face to free
his brow or cheek from the darkness. I never
saw his eyes, because Beerenbaum kept them
closed while he was thinking. For seconds at a
time the flickering light would distort his face
into grotesque grimaces, in which his nose was
suddenly double, or his chin and lower lip
disappeared, or his mouth looked like that of a
skull. Some afternoons I was unable to remember Beerenbaum's real face beneath the grimaces. So I invented another grimace against
the one I saw. The more I concentrated on
looking for Beerenbaum's real face in the
contours of his head, the greater and more
powerful became the silhouette-like body
behind the desk entwined in the hanging
branches of the copper beech. Beerenbaum's
silhouette in front of the window became
enormous, like a shadow that assumes ominous
dimensions the closer it gets to the light. This
must have been an illusion, for the lighting in
the room stayed the same.

Walking home in the evening through the
"village" after four or five hours of work for
Beerenbaum, I sometimes had the desire to

look in a mirror to see whether I still looked the same or whether I had adopted something of the Silent Close spirit world and its streets. I lit a cigarette as though exiting from a cinema at night, as if this proved that my participation in someone else's life story was now ended and my own life had begun again. When I turned into my street and saw Thekla Fleischer watering small fir trees that she raised on her balcony instead of flowers (she gave these as Christmas presents once they were too large for flower boxes), I remembered again that I wanted to learn the piano and that Herbert Beerenbaum was only an episode in my life that would end the moment he had dictated the last sentence of his memoirs.

*

"Madame Rosalie," the Count called, sliding with difficulty from the high barstool, "Madame Rosalie, what a pleasure to see you after this summer dry spell." The Count chuckled, because the allusion to the dry spell was supposed to be a witticism meaning the bar's early closing hours during vacation, of which today was the last day. The evening promised to turn into a riotous reunion of all the regulars, including the Count and Bruno. The Count's real name was Karl-Heinz Baron. Over ten years ago, this scholar, highly regarded by European experts in the field of Chinese language and literature, had been awarded the Pin of Honor for German-Soviet Friendship, which he called GESOV, for his work as treasurer of that association. Bruno had promptly elevated him to the title of Count in order to mitigate his shame.

The Count offered me his barstool. "We're expecting Brünoh," he said. "We're expecting...," he repeated, drawing out the syllables with a resonant promise, meaning that he was well aware of why I had come. Then he brought his head right up to my ear and whispered: "He's moved out of you-know-whose place, you know, I never could remember her name." Several weeks earlier, when I had run into the Count on Friedrichstrasse during my search for *Don Giovanni* paraphernalia, he had told me that Bruno had just moved in with a waitress. "No person of rank, no person of rank, if I understood correctly. Her shrill laugh, *igitt*, and the tendency to fullness in certain parts of her anatomy, it's quite indecent - bad, bad, bad." The Count shook his head, concerned, though he couldn't hide the lascivious gleam in his eyes. "Not at all a person of rank, and that for a man like Brünoh," the Count said again and quickly said goodbye, though not without gently kissing my hand.

"He's moved out now because he developed an allergy all of a sudden, they say, due to a cat living in the lady's house," the Count whispered, "but who can tell what causes an allergy. *Corpus nos veritatem cognoscere docet.* Oh, pardon me, Madame Rosalie, the body tells us the truth," he translated.

"Never mind," I said, and decided I had to learn the rudiments of Latin in addition to English, French, and the piano.

"I had a maternal aunt," the Count said, "who when she wished to obtain a divorce - we won't go into the question of guilt here - from a considerably older man, presented a medical report stating that she had a proven allergy against her husband's body perspiration. In point of fact, he suffered from disgusting, oozing rashes over his entire body. Because she was extremely wealthy, which was actually the *difficulté* with the divorce, they suspected my aunt of having bought the report and of wanting to leave her husband for a secret lover. This was as true as the fact that her own skin was flawless from the time she was granted the divorce to when she died at the age of ninety-two. Brünoh's body has simply corrected his tiny misdemeanor."

The Count enunciated Bruno's name with an even more pronounced French accent than usual, so as to preclude the slightest doubt of his undiminished esteem for Bruno.

I was grateful to the Count for going to such trouble to make up stories to console me, although I probably would never have found out about Bruno's affair with the waitress if he hadn't been so talkative. Though I considered the Count's theory about the possible cause of allergies to be wrong, I hoped he was right that Bruno's allergy was in fact directed at the waitress and not her cat. Bruno and I had been living apart for several months, though we couldn't agree who had left whom. While Bruno said I had left him, I was convinced I had been left by Bruno. As long as we were unsure of the exact circumstances of our parting or having been left, we could not really assume, or so I thought, that we had actually left each other.

The Count said he had bought another outfit yesterday - a pair of trousers, a frock coat, and two shirts, all very practical and inexpensive as well. His ladies had served him well.

Twice every year the Count went to a small men's outfitter near his apartment and let the sales girls there, whom he called "my ladies," talk him into buying the practical, inexpensive articles of clothing of which there were already dozens in his closet (he never threw anything away), differing from each other only in the degree to which they were too tight for the Count. That the Count called the unsightly jackets and pants made of a rubber-like, therefore wrinkle-free, material trousers and frock coat was his verbal tribute to a way of life that had remained his ideal, although he had never been able to implement it in his solitary existence. He was the son of wealthy parents, as he himself said, and had grown up with nannies and servants. His father traded in fabrics, uniform fabrics during the war, so that even at a time when his youngest brother was dying for want of his mother's milk fleeing with her through Pomerania, young Karl-Heinz Baron enjoyed the childhood of a born person of rank. Once the war was over his father disappeared somewhere west of the River Elbe, while his mother remained with her son in the city where they both had been born. Since then the Count's definition of the term "person of rank" has changed, so that when he uses it today, he actually means a person with manners.

Above all, a person of rank has to be educated, or if he lacks education, show proper respect for the education of others. Once a year, for his birthday, the Count permits himself a social attribute of a person of rank, that is, a servant who receives guests and serves them food. For this purpose he usually hires a certain Reinhold (whom Bruno calls Unhold, that is, monster), a tall, clumsy man from the neighborhood with the gaze of an animal, whom the Count forces to wear his tuxedo, whose sleeves reach no further than Reinhold's elbows. Reinhold's cousin had to fill in for him twice when Reinhold was in prison for having committed a crime (the Count didn't say what).

For the Count, the luxury of having a servant also included the right to bully him. For the hundred marks Reinhold was paid for his services, he had to allow himself to be patiently ordered around and corrected, to react obediently to every nervous gesture by the Count, and to place his left arm behind his back while decanting wine. Still Reinhold gave the impression of liking the role he had been given in his far-too-small tuxedo. I thought he might be pretending. Being afraid of him, I predicted the Count would die a violent death, perhaps by Reinhold's hand - after all, the murderer in Alfred Döblin's famous novel *Berlin Alexanderplatz* was also named Reinhold. Living as he did near Alexanderplatz (and it being very late), I attached particular significance to this fact.

The Count didn't seem to be frightened of

becoming a murder victim. I don't believe he excluded the possibility, though, because since then every time he said something about Reinhold, he called him his murderer. "My murderer helped me to carry a case of beer up the stairs yesterday," he said. The Count was one of the saddest people I knew, and sometimes I thought he really wouldn't care if Reinhold were to kill him one day. Several years ago, the Count, Bruno, and I were sitting together in a Pankow beergarden on a warm April day. The Count turned his face toward the sun - suddenly he looked like a very delicate, very old child. He said: "I don't know why, but I have to cry every May, with all the red flags and the first greenery. I have to cry when I see these two things together."

"Don't turn around, Madame Rosalie, do not turn around; he's here, Brünoh has come," the Count hissed from a narrow crack between his lips, staring at the entrance, looking over my head.

"With the waitress?" I asked.

"Alone, absolutely alone," the Count said.

"Then why shouldn't I turn around?"

"I shouldn't want to be too familiar with you, but I've noticed you always blush when you see him, and, pardon me, Madame Rosalie, a red face doesn't become you."

I asked myself why the Count was so concerned that I make a good impression on Bruno.

A hand brushed my shoulder and Bruno's voice said: "Evening, Rosa. Hello, Count."

"Two beers for Brünoh," the Count cried eagerly over the bar, as always when Bruno entered the bar sober. Bruno drank the first beer standing; the Count looked at him smiling, his head bent slightly back as if the beer were running down his own throat, not Bruno's.

Bruno drank the first two beers seriously but apathetically. They were for the road to the bar, the steps he had to climb in order to arrive in this noisy, stinking home for domesticated adventure. Only after these, when the ill-tempered shadows on his face were driven off by the hot redness, did he develop the qualities that raised him to the rank of a bar-room VIP, a title the Count had introduced years ago, one only he could grant or - this was rare - take away.

For the Count, Bruno was near the top of the hierarchy of bar-room VIPs. Bruno's presence and mood decided whether an evening would become a vulgar drinking bout or the beer would turn into a lake on which the Count and King Brünoh would steam up their fleets in staggered battle order, once again to amaze the meek race of the non-Latin drinkers.

With the anxious greed of a pourer who awaits the joy or displeasure of the one for whom he has poured, the Count probed the first effects of the beer on Bruno. I knew the game and contented myself with reading in the Count's expression what he saw on Bruno's face. It looked promising.

I could have left at this point. There was no room for me in Bruno's male life. I had tried to make the men who called each other Peti, Schmitti, Heinzi, Andi, or Manni, and whom Bruno called my "bar pals," forget the difference between them and me. I drank schnapps and beer with them instead of wine, I chummed up to them by butting into conversations about carburetor head seals and wood preservatives, I pretended to be passionately interested and, most of all, curious. I laughed at their jokes. But I always felt the effort it took them to talk to me. A sure sign of this was that the moment they turned to me they stopped using Berlin dialect, switching to standard German, as if I were a foreigner or a child to whom they had to talk slowly and distinctly. "You thirsty, yes?"

The bar is the last preserve of male freedom, Bruno would say. Which also means that women should keep their mouths shut in a real men's bar. Women upset the order every bar creates over time through the free interplay of forces, because, of course, no bar, and nothing else in the world for that matter, can manage without someone being in charge. In Bruno's bar the Latins ruled the non-Latins.

What rules in a bar, Bruno said, if it isn't a meeting place for pimps and cutthroats, is the thirst for interesting things. A drinker fears nothing more than boredom. The Latins contributed the most interesting part of the conversation, so domination quite naturally was theirs.

I considered Bruno's interpretation of the distribution of power in the bar to be idealized, because the Count, who was no less interesting than Bruno, indeed was sometimes even more interesting than Bruno, would never have managed to dominate the carpenters, circus performers, and stage crew members alone, without Bruno's help, if only because of his drooping shoulders and soft, almost feminine hips. More crucial than the Latins' erudition was Bruno's open, fighting spirit, which struck him at a high level of blood alcohol. Like a frozen June bug that puts out its feelers and tries its wings when you breathe on it, Bruno began to rock one knee, stretch his neck, and start looking for victims.

Some days he was content to end the others'

stories with associations or quotes that destroyed the storyteller's intent in a few seconds,
garnering Bruno the approving laughter of the
listeners. Other days he looked for an argument. Then his rocking thigh would start to
vibrate and all that was needed was an innocuous remark such as 'Peti gave his wife a clock
for her birthday' to unleash a haughty attack
against birthdays, marriages, gifts - especially
against clocks as gifts - that could end in a
philosophical discourse on the world of owner-
ship, the big bang, and the fourth dimension.

I've never seen Bruno lose an argument,
even the most idiotic. And no one held his
victories against him. Having a low opinion of
their own mental powers, the losers would have
been hurt if Bruno, their genius Bruno, were to
lose.

Bruno said, "Well, Rosa, how does it feel
living the life of the Statue of Liberty?"

"Oh, oh, oh," the Count whispered behind
Bruno's back, shaking his hand as if he had
burned himself.

"Good," I said and gave up my idea of
talking to Bruno about Beerenbaum, which is
why I had come to the bar.

The longer I worked for Beerenbaum the
stronger my feeling grew of doing something
forbidden. As I wrote down what Beerenbaum

dictated without contradiction, I asked myself more and more whether I wasn't becoming an accomplice by helping him forge a monument to himself in letters. The fact that Beerenbaum was growing used to me, that he even seemed happy to see me on Tuesdays and Fridays, made things worse, especially since in order to justify my being his accomplice I had to consider myself a spy who had to fathom Beerenbaum's sleeping habits and illnesses, his tastes, his favorite food, his secret thoughts, his tics and sensitivities, like someone who had to study his victim painstakingly in order to plan a perfect murder.

Bruno sat on the barstool, his elbows propped against the bar, and swung his leg. "Rosa," he said, "you ought to be fair. We've let you watch our experiment in living for years as an audience. Isn't that right, Count?"

"You really can't deny that, Madame Rosalie."

"We let you witness Meier drink himself into a cirrhosis, Kurti run to Alcoholics Anonymous..."

"And Cliffi get cliffier and cliffier, to the point that he's now close to being *non compos mentis*," the Count interrupted.

Cliffi owed his name to a character in "Dallas," an especially foolish man named Cliff

Barnes. The Count - he had been the first to notice the similarity - immediately, joyfully spread this huge sensation to the bar. "Have you noticed how much our W. looks like Cliff Barnes," he whispered to everyone, including me, again and again. Since then he always called W. "Cliff," also introducing the word *cliffy* as a synonym for stupid.

"I have to admit Cliffi has recently become so cliffy I find him almost unbearable," the Count said. "He's almost become a problem of rank, Brünoh."

Cliff, a chemist with a PhD, was one of the Latins, although he knew no more Latin than what was absolutely essential for his field, like all other Latins except the Count and Bruno, the two for whom the carpenters and stage hands had named the clique.

"Did you hear that, Rosa," Bruno said, "we even let you observe Cliffi's cliffication, but you want to experiment out of public view."

"Nothing's happened," I said. "The piano teacher is still in love."

"Rosa," Bruno said, reaching for his third beer, "you became independent one year ago. What are you doing there, what are you doing in freedom, tell us that, Rosa."

"A retiree from the neighborhood is dictating his family history for his grandchildren. He had a stroke and his right hand is paralyzed," I said, in the suspicion that Bruno would want more information.

He squinted, suspiciously. "What kind of retiree can afford that sort of luxury?"

"He was a doctor," I said, "it's not really very interesting, a kind of genealogical research." Then, to put Bruno on the wrong track, I asked whether he knew why *Don Giovanni* is so seldom sung in German.

Bruno slid down from his barstool. "Did you hear that, Count? Rosa is interested in opera. She was never interested in opera. So that's what you do now that you're free, something as wonderful as becoming interested in opera." Bruno swung his beer glass like a trophy. "To freedom. Long live freedom."

The false assumption that I was now interested in opera sent Bruno into an apotheosis of freedom.

"Ah, Count, think of all the things we could do if we were free."

"True freedom has no shape and can only be found behind prison walls," the Count quoted in a tone of voice that tolerated no contradiction, not even from Bruno. For a few moments we thought about the three years the Count had spent in jail. It had been almost twenty-five years since they had locked up the Count.

Bruno was the first one who dared to speak. "You are right, Count, freedom is not a place. But what if it were a place?"

"I think," I said, "freedom is as much a place as a human being is a place."

Bruno groaned. The Count, apparently regretting his bluntness, said cautiously, "Of course, one mustn't forget that people are concrete, while freedom, on the other hand, is an abstraction."

"Enough philosophizing, Rosa," said Bruno.

I would liked to have added that abstract freedom can exist in concrete humans like a pocket of air in amber; after all, the air was still only air, without the amber. I dropped the idea because I assumed Bruno and the Count would ruin this fine thought with their pure philosophy and because, when all was said and done, I really didn't care. I was neither interested in opera nor in the place Bruno thought freedom was. I was interested in Beerenbaum, but I couldn't talk about him.

"Let's return to something solid," Bruno said. "Freedom is awareness of necessity. *Ergo*: another beer, please."

I told Bruno I would get in touch with him over the next few days, then let the Count kiss my hand, and left.

Once home I took an open bottle of wine

out of the refrigerator and sat down in one of the six black chairs I had bought from Peti. A cousin of Peti's who lived in the West had given them to him for his fortieth birthday. They had chrome-plated tubular steel frames and soft cushions with coarse wool covers. Two weeks later Peti complained that the black things depressed him. Then when he found out that the chairs were made in the East and sold at a low price by IKEA in the West, he vented his anger at both the East and his stingy cousin on the chairs, calling them "black beasts." He probably secretly kicked them, too. One day he asked whether anyone wanted these beasts at two hundred marks apiece. I took them.

I sat at the table with five black chairs, drank wine, and did nothing else. Five black chairs like five headless men in black suits with black shoes were sitting all around me as if they were going to bury me. Like they were now burying Beerenbaum. All of us dressed in black, wearing black shoes. Except that Beerenbaum, invisible between silk cushions under the coffin lid, was wearing his dove-grey suit.

But this evening I sat between five headless men disguised as black chairs, who were going to bury me, and drank wine. "Cheers, gentlemen, fill your throats if you don't have mouths."

I raised my glass. The five remained silent and motionless. This did not bother me. I just asked myself whether they were five complete strangers, perhaps also hostile to me, who had sneaked into my house by way of Peti to try out their powers of depressing people once Peti had got wind of their ambush. This is what I thought as I emptied the bottle. When I got up to fetch the next bottle from the kitchen, I noticed it - a pale violet cosmea - had separated from the bouquet in the white vase on the table by twisting its stem and was bending in my direction. I had changed the water for the flowers that afternoon and rearranged them; I hadn't noticed anything so strange as this. I attributed this unusual activity to the flower's longing for light and devoted myself to the next bottle of wine.

There were nights when ghosts came to my apartment. A sudden rustling in a corner, or a curtain moving without a window or door being open; something tapped me on the shoulder without showing itself. Sometimes I also distinctly felt someone sit down next to me and remain sitting quietly. In that case I would feel relieved, as it had come to protect me. I knew I was neither particularly happy nor sober whenever such strange things happened.

I sat between the five black men and tried to

fathom whether their presence had anything to do with Beerenbaum, whether they had appeared as a warning to show me what I had stooped to, or whether they simply wanted to be malicious by demonstrating that I was alone at night. I thought that I would have been better off not bringing the black beasts into my house, that I would ask Bruno to buy them from me.

At that moment something brushed against my skin, as gently as a daddy longlegs, as delicately as a butterfly at rest. It was the cosmea that was meanwhile so far from its fellow flowers that it reached my left arm resting on the table. My original supposition, that the flower was moving toward the light, turned out to be groundless, because it had distinctly turned away from the source of light and bent down to my arm.

Although cosmea is usually fructose, with one plant bearing ten, twenty or more blossoms, the one bending toward me was a single blossom on a thin, straight stem. I didn't dare move my arm touched by the tips of the lower leaves as it turned its tiny yellow face in the middle of the violet wreath toward me. It behaved strangely, like someone under hypnosis.

"What do you want," I asked. I wouldn't have been surprised if it had really answered me. It did not. But I could swear that it turned its head a bit higher so we could look each other straight in the eye, if it had had eyes.

"Listen," I said, "tell me what you want." I could have sworn it was looking at me, it was asking me to do something, but what? Maybe it wanted to drink something other than water. I dipped my index finger in the wineglass and tapped it right in the middle of the yellow face.

"Cheers," I said, and took a sip.

It had extended its delicate stem in a straight line, transformed every turn into length such that I had the impression it had grown an inch or two in several minutes. I slowly thought I understood - it wanted to reach me, that was all.

I knew my question was blunt, still I asked: "Do you love me?" I quickly checked the reaction of the five black men. They stood in the room around the table - five normal, not particularly ugly chairs. We were alone now, the cosmea and me. "Are you a man," I asked. "Is your name Cosmea or Cosmos?"

It didn't answer, so I fell back on one of my pet ideas that we all have to be plant, animal, and human. I couldn't decide on the order, though I considered only two variations probable: plant, animal, human, or human, animal, plant.

I discarded the possibility of a direct kinship between plant and human. However, the similarity between various types of people with birds, apes, frogs, rabbits, cats, pigs, and all sorts of other animals was so obvious that my intuition of a mysterious phylogenetic if not ontogenetic link grew greater with the years, becoming certainty on nights like this. Not even someone who loved him could have denied Beerenbaum resembled a salientia. I had no idea what Beerenbaum had looked like as a young man, but I assumed the salientia in him was hidden in the hints of wrinkles, especially around his mouth and chin, like a picture puzzle. The question was: did Beerenbaum's human life serve to prepare him for his existence as a salientia and was this why he looked more and more like his coming form of existence as he grew older, or was he dragging his long-forgotten life as salientia through this one, as we all do, unaware?

"Were you a human, or are you going to become a human?" I asked my cosmea, who now seemed relaxed and satisfied since I had devoted my attention to it. It even attempted to bend its stem again slightly. "Cheers, dear girl," I said. "It's a pity, you know something and can't say it; I could say it but don't know it."

This was the thought my drunk brain offered as the key to the secret.

Of course, it was quite simple, they have thought up the sneakiest and meanest variation for us. First human, then animal, then plant. The deeper we penetrate the secret the less we can say about it. It's that simple. So I still had two lives before me. I hoped I wouldn't have to become a house pet, a hamster on a wheel, or a pig for slaughter. The thought of a banal life as a cauliflower or chives made me sad. I wished that the cosmea hadn't enlightened me about the horrible, silent future awaiting me.

It lightly swayed its stem, which could have meant all sorts of things. I was too tired to understand it. "Good night," I said. "All the best. Maybe you'll become wind and we'll meet again." Then I kissed it.

*

An average-looking, grey-haired man in the first row got up and moved forward with short steps, purposefully, as if he knew exactly the spot where he had to stop. He bowed to the coffin or to Beerenbaum's portrait, and said, "Dear Herbert." I glanced at the musicians' faces. They looked as though they hadn't heard anything. Or they thought it was normal for a man to address a coffin or a photograph as "dear Herbert." I was convinced all of Beerenbaum's mourners were atheists. All the more so this man, who had been given a seat in the first row and presumably would soon be delivering a speech. Why - except that he believed Beerenbaum's soul was hovering somewhere between or above us, perhaps even quite properly above his mortal remains, listening to us - why else would he say "dear Herbert" to a planed piece of wood. Apparently, even staunch atheists could not resist the mystical force of death. The man turned to those seated. He had a fat, shiny face, half of which consisted of a colossal double fold in which his chin sat like a well-healed scar. The double chin spilled over his broad lower jaw and neck down to his upper chest. It was the most impressive double chin I had ever seen, although I had long been interested in the psychological significance of double chins. There were natural and unnatural double chins. The natural ones were the result of gluttony, alcoholism, age, or nature, and in most cases they were a harmonious part of the expression and form of the face as a whole. Danton or Bach would be inconceivable without a double chin, just as Jesus Christ would be with one. The natural double chin makes no demands on our experience of the human face;

often as not, we don't even notice it. The unnatural double chin, on the other hand, immediately causes the curious observer to ask how this pouch of flesh came into being.

After years of observation I found out that unnatural double chins are exclusively the product of unnatural professions; and since there were virtually no natural professions left anymore, these must be particularly unnatural professions. On my way to the Barabas institute, which had taken me along the banks of the River Spree past the rear entrance of Friedrichstrasse Station for over fifteen years, except for Sundays and holidays, I had come across countless men in uniform with this kind of double chin, without my being able to explain where they had gotten this physiological blunder. Nothing in the faces of these men indicated debauched epicureanism. Most of them were young and their skin firm enough to keep in form even if moderately overweight. I found the explanation for the phenomenon on the train to Bulgaria. Just such young men - they all look strangely alike - were checking passports. They wore a small folding lectern around their necks where they put the passports, they carefully turned the pages, and finally stamped them. Their job required them constantly to press their chin against their chest, as if they had to spend the whole day looking at the tips of their toes. If they had humbly bent their shoulders and necks, nothing would have happened. But as their bodies also had to serve as symbols of state authority, they were forced, against all anatomical common sense, to keep their stomach and chest perpendicular, head bent down at a right angle, creating even in thin men a bulge between chin and neck that slowly gelled into an unnatural double chin if held over long periods of time.

The man with the most unnatural double chin I had ever seen was talking about Beerenbaum's childhood in the Ruhr and his sure class instinct in almost exactly the same words Beerenbaum had dictated to me. I was waiting for the sentence with the little lad: "Even as a little lad I knew..." The double chin sat bulging and pink on the man's rump. Above it, exactly in the middle of his head, was a small, round, muscular opening - his mouth. He knew early in life that his heart was on the left and the enemy on the right, he said. He had cut the "little lad."

I assumed that the man had gone to primary school with Beerenbaum or had worked with him, and been equally successful; perhaps this was even his successor. In either case he knew the memoirs, which was why Beerenbaum was now delivering his own funeral oration.

The hard period of emigration full of privation, the man said. No mention of the Hotel Lux. As he spoke, the double chin swelled like that of a gobbling turkey. I couldn't help staring fixedly at this pouch of flesh, and the longer I stared at it the bigger it seemed to get. What if it burst, I thought, like a bloated frog? Did a double chin ever burst? What was inside a bulging, ham-hock-colored double chin like this? Then it happened: the worms in my paternal grandmother began wallowing in a mixture of fatty tissue, blood, and pieces of skin. I closed my eyes, opened them as wide as I could, looked at the musicians, hoping their indifference could make the disgusting image disappear. I avoided looking at the speaker's face. No good - fat, plump, white worms fell out of the split double chin.

My stomach started to throb. It was trying to empty itself through spasmodic upward motion. I wiped the cold sweat from my brow. I remembered the crumpled newspaper in my coat pocket. But I couldn't publicly vomit into newspaper during Beerenbaum's funeral just because the speaker had a double chin. What could I do to get rid of this disgusting feeling? I had to think of something else, but how? I unbuttoned my coat and pressed against my stomach with the palm of my hand.

> *Era già alquanto*
> *Avanzata la notte,*
> *Quando nelle mie stanze, ove soletta*
> *Mi trovai per sventura....a*

I had no idea what these verses meant, but I had heard *Don Giovanni* so many times by now that I could sing along with most of the arias in Italian.

> *...entrar io vidi*
> *In un mantello avvolto*
> *Un uom che al primo istante*
> *Avea preso per voi;*
> *Ma riconobbi poi*
> *Che un inganno era il mio...*

I sang silently against the double chin and the awful feeling in my stomach. I sang and I heard myself sing. I had the voice of Birgit Nilsson. My singing coursed through my body like blood, into my arms, legs, head, and stomach, so loud, so impetuously that all I could hear was my own wonderful Nilsson voice and Donna Anna's lament.

*

I woke up with a headache and the vague memory of a threatening dream. It was Friday, market day and Beerenbaum day. I had already been working for Beerenbaum for six weeks; more and more I regretted having gotten involved in the business. I was strictly observing my resolution to exclude my brain from all gainful employment by not telling Beerenbaum what I thought about him and his memoirs. But I couldn't prevent myself from thinking about the fact that I grappled with Beerenbaum mentally all day and half the night.

During our last session he had dictated the following sentence: "Supported by the rich experience of the Leninist Party and its fraternal assistance, our Party led the working class to victory, building socialism for all time in the first workers' and peasants' state upon German soil." A perfectly ordinary sentence, just one of thousands written and spoken; with time they became no more conspicuous than the number of grey hairs on the head of a person one sees every day. But I had to write this sentence with my own hands. I was paid money for writing it down. If I hadn't been certain Beerenbaum was expecting me to contradict him, I would at least have asked him about one of the five lies the sentence contained.

It was Friday, Beerenbaum day. As I was eating breakfast, I analyzed the dream that had left behind a sticky, uneasy feeling in me. The memory of it floated around the room like a ghost; no sooner had I approached it than it scattered into nothingness. I took a pill for my headache. It was ten-thirty. Four and a half hours until I started working for Beerenbaum.

I was just getting ready to draw myself a hot bath when the doorbell rang. It was Irma returning from the market. "You've still got time," she said, putting her shopping bag down next to the refrigerator. I bought stewed cucumbers with tomatoes, my kids really like stewed cucumbers with tomatoes. Do you like stewed cucumbers with tomatoes, too?" Irma asked, as she resolutely marched down the corridor into the room. I walked behind her. She dropped into the black chairs with a sigh. Irma looked plump but she wasn't fat. Still she took up three chairs by herself. Whenever Irma sat at my table she filled three chairs. There was no way you could sit in the chair to the left or right of the one Irma was in. She put an arm over the back of the left chair, while she placed the bent knee of the leg whose ankle rested on her other thigh on the seat of the right chair. I thought it must be difficult to sit like that. Irma didn't.

"I have to talk to somebody," Irma said. "You have no idea how depressed I am."

I assumed she was as depressed as every other time she rang my bell. Irma didn't visit me unless she was depressed. I found out during one of her recent depressions that she had had a party with a few friends two days before when she was feeling really good. I might even have hated Irma.

"I think it's terrible. Don't you think it's terrible," Irma said.

"What," I asked.

"Don't you listen to the news? They said on the news that they've started shooting again on the Sino-Russian border. It means war, that's for sure."

Irma took one of my cigarettes.

"I'm absolutely sure this means war," she said, and opened the inner two-thirds of her wide mouth, keeping the corners of her mouth firmly closed. Irma was the only person I knew who talked like this; it meant that what was being told went without saying, so it wasn't worth opening her mouth completely.

Irma had announced the outbreak of a Sino-Russian war a number of times, so I refrained from looking surprised, which Irma interpreted as stupidity. She opened her entire mouth to a broad smile baring her upper teeth from her gums, and said: "I don't think you understood me: *this means war*. The Russians need an enemy now. They can't feed them-selves, it's unbelievable, but they can't feed

themselves, you see?" Irma was still smiling.
"They don't dare come to Europe, so they have
to start a war with China. It's perfectly clear."
Irma shook her big head with the crazy curls,
intensified her smile to a deep, sympathetic
laugh, and said, "Well, I can't tell you how clear
that is to me."

Irma attributed her profound knowledge of
Russian policy to her Russian grandmother,
who had come to Berlin during the twenties as
a drama student, where she married a German.
The Russian blood in her, Irma claimed, gave
her a more profound understanding of the
Russian soul than that of the rational Germans.

"Do you really think this means war?" I
asked.

"What else?" Irma said with a squeaky
chuckle; she closed the corners of her mouth
again. "Yes, really, truly. If I didn't have kids
I'd kill myself. I can't bear it, this constant
waiting for it to start. And you can't even
emigrate, to New Zealand or Australia. Even
my kids have started dreaming about war."

I didn't tell her that I never dreamed about
war. I simply couldn't understand why people
were more afraid of universal death than of
their own. As though it were easier to die
alone. To wake up at night, to understand that
you had to die now, alone, without saying

farewell, no one to swear a lie about the hereafter, no one to say, perhaps we'll meet again - that would be a horrible death.

My headache went from the back of my neck into my shoulders. I did not know how to comfort Irma. "You can still kill yourself once the war starts, you know," I said.

"Don't you have any imagination," Irma asked, "or aren't you interested?"

"I'm serious," I said. "As long as we live, we know we're going to die, and still we don't kill ourselves, at least most of us don't . . . Irma," I said, "I have a horrible headache."

Irma pulled up her knee and her extended arm. "I think we're all going to go crazy, don't you think we're all going to go crazy? Wouldn't that be funny: we all go crazy and don't even notice it because we all slowly go crazy together, so no one could notice it."

"That would be pretty funny," I said.

Irma suddenly became still and fit into one chair. Her skirt had slid over her skinny knees - at which her otherwise fleshy and column-shaped legs were usually bent slightly inwards - overly large, touching child's legs that looked even clumsier owing to Irma's predilection for loud, red, high-heeled shoes. It was always like this with Irma - either I hated her or I felt sorry for her.

"Would you like some tea," I asked.

"I have to cook stewed cucumbers with tomatoes for the kids; I'm all right again, really. The best thing would be for us all to go crazy, don't you think that'd be best?"

I said that I thought it would be best too and thought I'd go crazy on the spot if she didn't leave.

Once she had closed the door after herself, I resolved not to open it again until I had to leave the apartment to begin working for Beerenbaum. If I had been able to decide to go to the market after all, if I had forgotten Irma and her crude ideas, I wouldn't have had the argument with Beerenbaum. But that's what Irma was like: she withdrew like a sated vampire and I was left drained. Irma's idea, that we would all slowly go mad without noticing it, accompanied me all the way to Beerenbaum's door. It was Friday; Beerenbaum opened the door. He was wearing a dark blue cardigan I hadn't yet seen over a light blue shirt, grey trousers, and, instead of his usual Bordeaux-red leather slippers, black tie shoes. He smiled when he said hello. He was in a good mood, as if something very pleasant had happened to him or he was expecting it to. I still had a headache, and Beerenbaum's open cheerfulness irritated me.

He must have looked like this when his hand wasn't shaking, when he signed promotions and dismissals, pounded imperiously on conference tables, or shook hands with other powerful men. Beerenbaum was indestructible, he was blessed with eternal life.

"Nice of you to come," he said; "I am also expecting an unusual guest. We will start work a bit later than usual today."

He led me into the living room, where he had received me the first time and I had not entered since.

"I'm going to have to take advantage of you today, Miss Polkowski, but don't be afraid, there's no mental work involved, no mental work. A writer, Victor Sensmann, will be coming shortly. They say he writes interesting books. I haven't read them myself, but they tell me they're good. I want you to take notes on what we say."

"You don't trust him?" I asked.

"You have to be careful with artists; they like to use artistic freedom as an excuse. Do you know something by him?"

I had read two of his books, light political novels that owed their success to being considered daring, though falsely so. Sensmann told commonly known secrets so seriously you couldn't help thinking he had hidden another, a real secret, beneath them. I said I had heard of Sensmann but hadn't read anything by him.

Beerenbaum asked me to help him set the coffee table. With his left hand he opened a glass door of the wall unit containing a Meissen coffee service with a grapevine pattern.

"Three cups and all that goes with them," he said, then walked into the kitchen to put on the water for coffee. His gait was faster and more controlled than previous times.

Beerenbaum and I set the coffee table together for a guest we were both expecting. I noticed my routine movements. Saucers, cups, where are the coffee spoons? This is how I used to set the coffee table with my mother on Sundays while my father was still alive. An obscene familiarity, a forbidden normality was growing between me and Beerenbaum.

Finally, the doorbell rang. Beerenbaum took his time for the few steps to the front door, as if he wanted to avoid the impression that he was impatiently awaiting his guest.

Victor Sensmann looked like the photos I had seen of him: pale face with wide jaw bones, the skin around his small eyes wrinkled from constant smiling, high eyebrows beneath a wrinkled brow, everything about him showed the exertion of having to create an interested, pensive impression every second. He wore jeans and an earth-colored woolen jacket with leather elbow patches. Beerenbaum introduced me as his right hand and demonstrated the fact by placing the trembling lump of flesh I had to replace on the table.

"He doesn't trust artists," I said, to explain my presence.

"Quite right, quite right," Sensmann said hastily, though it wasn't clear whether he was agreeing with Beerenbaum or threatening him.

I poured the coffee. Sensmann thanked me by quickly moving his eyes. He said he had come to find out about Beerenbaum's fascinating life. I thought that was overdoing things, but excusable; after all he had to get Beerenbaum into the proper mood, if needs be flatter him, if he wanted to find something out. I was even willing to interpret his exaggerated politeness - he began almost every sentence with "Herr Professor" - as irony or as a sign of aloof contempt. Beerenbaum, however, saw this as respect. You didn't have to see Sensmann in person to know he was no rebel. His books contained not rebels, but defenseless creatures with dried-up souls. So much so that after reading them I had to ask myself how he could stand the company of these people without creating a rebel for or against them during the writing. He was much thinner than I had imagined him; in fact, he was all skin and bones - he held his emaciated limbs in front of him at various angles, making him look like a collapsible garden chair. I found him touching, and although I was rather repelled by his weak figure and its reflection in his books, I could not bear to think that he thought about me the way I thought about the housekeeper: as Beerenbaum's loyal creature. I felt the urge to let him know that, in case he wanted an ally against Beerenbaum, he could count on me.

Half an hour later I was screaming between the highly polished set of cupboards and the furniture covered in satin, calling Sensmann a disgusting bootlicker and Beerenbaum a thick-headed big shot, whose lackey I wouldn't be for another second. The cause of my anger - I was ashamed of my childish fit even as I threw it - was ridiculous, as ridiculous as the assumption that a man like Victor Sensmann needed my support, even if he was as thin as Christ on the cross.

Sensmann had said he was working on a novel about university life in Berlin during the early sixties; since Beerenbaum had held an important function at the university during that period, he hoped to find out some otherwise unobtainable background information from him. While Sensmann was still talking, a smugness spread over Beerenbaum's face of someone who is about to vouchsafe his interviewer an answer. "As you can imagine, those were exciting times just after the construction of our anti-Fascist rampart," he said.

The effrontery of having to write down these words, as if they were words like flower, dog, or wall, enraged me.

I noted: "B: period after construction of the anti-Fascramp was exciting."

Sensmann said he was fourteen at the time, which could mean that he was either too young to remember or old enough to remember well. The bare fact that Sensmann was twenty-four years younger than he was now seemed too insignificant to write down.

"Back then," Beerenbaum said, "before the historic month of August '61, I often had a vision when looking down Unter den Linden as I entered the University, a vision of streams of the lifeblood of the young Republic, red and pulsating, flowing through the Brandenburg Gate straight into the greedy body of the enemy."

Sensmann said nothing and lit a cigarette; he looked at me as he let out the smoke from his first puff. This glance together with the relaxed exhalation like a sigh, lulled me into believing he wanted to signal to me he was relieved to have found someone who shared his views. I even imagined I saw a call for help in Sensmann's eyes. Sensmann could not openly oppose Beerenbaum, and he wanted me to help him.

"So you preferred to make the blood flow yourself by building a wall where you could shoot the necessary openings in people's bodies," I said.

For two or three seconds it was as quiet as if all three of us had held our breath. Then Beerenbaum said, smiling at Victor Sensmann: "Yes, Miss Polkowski, we also had to fight views like yours at the University at the time."

Sensmann said to Beerenbaum in a tone of voice that sounded as if two reasonable grown-ups were coming to an agreement behind the back of a stubborn child: "I also believe it was a necessary decision."

I threw my pencil at the Meissen porcelain with the grapevine pattern and screamed.

*

As a child I had the misfortune of having a father who was both my school principal (this was dictated by school zoning) and teacher. My father tried several times to spare me, but most of all himself, this torture. According to the implacable will of the authorities, however, we were chained to each other outside the household for more than ten years.

My father's absence during the first seven years of my life meant that Ida and my mother had to see to my upbringing. My father intervened only when he thought he had to defend my mother against me or, more frequently, in matters of political education. He would sit down next to me at the round dining room table with the blue polka dot cloth and talk about the bulwark of socialism defying war-mongering imperialism, the glorious Communist struggle for the final liberation of mankind, the last drops of blood and sacred dead he too had taken an oath to defend. He was more interesting when he told about how he had gotten into fights with high school students as a working-class boy. He called this "my school of class struggle." He always paused before saying "high school" and "high school students" as if collecting saliva in his mouth, which he would then contemptuously spit out.

It didn't matter what he talked about. He simply sat down next to me at the table, alone, and directed his words at me. I usually paid little attention to what he said; instead I concentrated on convincing him I was listening. I tried to look attentive and intelligent, nodding in agreement from time to time so as not to discourage him. In spite of this, his pedagogical efforts never lasted longer than twenty minutes. He would place both of his hands on the edge of the table, push himself back, and say: "Well, time to get back to work," and go into the study.

I thought of questions I assumed would please him. How often is a genius like Stalin born? Every hundred, perhaps only every two hundred years. Do murderers still exist under Communism? No, there are no murderers under Communism. These were the wrong questions; the answers were too easy. I still stood expectantly next to the dining room table after he had left the room.

I began to think of questions he couldn't dismiss in a single sentence, in the space of four or five steps as he walked past me; and I discovered something that would have changed my childhood, youth, and heaven knows what else. I had worked a week on this question. I was certain that it would impress him, and it was complicated enough for a long talk at the dining room table. I waited for an evening when my mother came home later and when no one would take his mind off me and my question. The two of us were eating supper. He was eating an open-face tomato sandwich. "If the working class is the most progressive class," I said, "it was also the only class that could have prevented Fascism. Why didn't the working class do that?" He had lost all his teeth to scurvy as a prisoner of war. When he ate bread he would often run his tongue between his dentures and gums to lick away the crumbs. He would raise his upper lip high above his lower one in such a way that he appeared to bear his teeth in anger. After he finally swallowed his food, he asked who had told me such nonsense.

Things couldn't have been worse. Not only did he not like the question, he even doubted it was mine. I came to my defense, though I don't remember how. My father was convinced I was a victim of enemy propaganda, though he could not explain to me who except the working class could have stopped Fascism.

"Do you mean to say that the victim, not the wrongdoer is guilty?" my father yelled.

"If the victim does not fight back, he also bears part of the guilt," I yelled back. I fought for the guilt of victims as if I were fighting for my life. The passion of that evening had such an effect on me that to this day I refuse to equate victims with innocence, which sometimes leads me to think dangerous thoughts.

Most of all, though, I learned that day that I could arouse my father's interest in me only by asking him questions he did not like. We argued about the guilt of the working class until my mother came home and broke us up.

Having been unable to please him, from that point on I thought only about how to displease him. I stopped asking about the heroic deeds of Communists; I doubted them. I no longer had him explain to me what it meant that someone said there was no freedom of thought. I said that myself. My parents could only explain the appalling change in my political views through enemy influences in my immediate vicinity. Suspicion fell on my class, and my father, the principal, took steps to counter the ideological subversion of 7B.

Starting immediately, class began with going over the papers, and each teacher was, apparently, asked to convey part of his knowledge along with the appropriate political interpretation. Mathematics was not simply mathematics; in the hands of the class enemy mathematics was an instrument of oppression by the ruling class, as were biology, chemistry, and sports.

I was in a terrible position. My very existence made me guilty, me the principal's daughter, because of whom the whole class was subjected to pedagogical torture simply because she argued with her parents.

Moreover, I could see the mistrust in the

eyes of my classmates, who had to assume that I had denounced them. In order to be rehabilitated, I had to protest against educational methods more vehemently than all the others and regale teachers with underhanded questions more often. To survive in my class I had to lead the resistance.

I was thirteen. I had managed to arouse my father's interest in me. Sometimes, before falling asleep, I wished he was dead.

That year the senior school authorities instructed my father to hold five rehearsals for the May Day parade because our school - my school and my father's - had put on a disgracefully undisciplined, unmilitary performance the year before. At home my father exploded. The school inspector, he said, is a silly goose, a stupid goat. He had no talent for verbal abuse, in fact he had no talent at all. "After all," he said, "I'm not a drill sergeant and the school isn't basic training. I'll have to think of something." He didn't think of anything. So we marched. Along Kurt-Fischer-Strasse, past the Schönholz Heath to the cemetery where we are now burying Beerenbaum, and back, every afternoon from Tuesday to Saturday: it rained on Saturday. During the march along Kurt-Fischer-Strasse, at about where the writer Stephan Hermlin lives, the group - I had been appointed right flank - decided to end the torture by running away. We waited for a small path, to which a barely visible cave-like entrance led which other children had created in the thick bushes between the street and the Schönholz Heath. Once inside we disappeared as quickly and quietly as Indians, and if Renchen Baude hadn't reported us to the school principal, our flight would probably have had no consequences. But Renchen Baude did report us, not (as she claimed to us) because she disapproved of what we had done, but because we had left the others, including Renchen Baude, in the lurch. The renegades decided that the principal's daughter had the least to fear, so I was given the role of instigator, which I gladly accepted because it gave me an opportunity to prove I really was one of them and that I didn't give a damn about the school, my father, or my mother. I didn't give a damn about anything that could make me suspicious in their eyes.

This put me in the triangle between van Gogh's *Sunflowers*, my father, and my mother. Everyone stared at me - the flowers unperturbed, my father full of hatred, my mother in despair. They all agreed. My father agreed with the school inspector, who was no longer a silly goose; he even agreed with Renchen Baude, even though she was a bad student; my mother agreed with my father, because he was right; the *Sunflowers* hung on the wall and were part of things. An iron unity I had created because of something I did not understand; I didn't have a clue how to fight it and I howled.

I recognized this unity again between Sensmann and Beerenbaum: the strict observance of rules arising from interests. This time I was the servant of this unity instead of its victim. And once again I suddenly found myself between the cabinets and the furniture, and I howled. "Don't you know we're all slowly going mad without noticing it?" I cried. "Hasn't anyone heard the news? There's a war, yes, there's a war going on between a bunch of insane people who don't know they've gone mad." I yelled other things, too, though I can't remember what.

When I slammed the door behind me, there was a crimson-red car in front of the house, and a tall thin man walked through the front yard. He had a pale, almost white face, with two grey, motionless eyes so dull and glazed they either saw nothing or everything. I was either so excited, or the headache that was still tormenting the right half of my brain, or perhaps Irma's visit had such an effect on me that I thought I had looked death in the face. This was the first time I saw Michael Beerenbaum.

The only sound was the rustling of withered leaves under my feet. The "village" lay lifeless in the October haze. The invisible dwellers had hoisted flags on the flagpoles in their front yards, which hung slack in the still air. I walked along the roadway, close to the gutter where the wind had piled the leaves, dragging my feet in the rotting leaves until I had left the "village" semicircle and the cars forced me onto the sidewalk. It all belongs to them, I thought, the paving stones, the houses, the trees, the light behind the windows. It all belongs to Beerenbaum and this man with the dead eyes; it probably also belongs to Sensmann. I belonged to them too as soon as I entered this house, the accursed house at Silent Close No. 6, with its Persian carpets and floral-pattern curtains, its wall units, corner units, and the rusty birch wood on the wall instead of van Gogh's *Sunflowers*.

It made no sense to turn the lights on once I got home. I sat on one of the black chairs and imagined how ugly and ridiculous I must have looked when I behaved like a petulent child in front of Sensmann and Beerenbaum. Everything you do is wrong, I thought, you always do the wrong thing. Every step I take ends in a mistake, every flick of the wrist is wrong. What kind of world is this where you can't do anything right? My Aunt Ida, for example, who spent thirty years of her life earning a small income buying notebooks, dolls in folk costumes, nutcrackers, and decorative plates for a society, The Society for Understanding between Peoples, that gave them to its friends abroad. The name promised only good. What could be wrong about buying little dolls in folk costumes to make someone happy? When I told Ida that I had heard that the Society for Understanding between Peoples was a subsidiary of the secret police, she laughed, and said she always said that people see ghosts, and continued buying this junk till the day she died. Who could know the damage Ida's little dolls in folk costumes had done? Just suppose they were given to some American of German ancestry in Lexington, Kentucky. All German Americans are interested in their genealogy; this one's forefathers emigrated to America from Mecklenburg, say, two hundred years ago. The man from Lexington, Kentucky, had inherited an attachment to Mecklenburg, which was so intensified by the doll (in Mecklenburg dress, of course) that the man was prepared to find out the name of the odds-on favorite in the Kentucky Derby, which he then betrayed to the carrier of the little doll. The Bulgarian secret police, in turn, could use one of its poison-tipped umbrellas against this favored horse - a horse with a future as brilliant as that of the legendary Man o' War, so that the Russian stallion Anilin, bearer of the Soviet Medal for Bravery, could be assured of victory at the Kentucky Derby. Ida would have been an accomplice to this crime, even though she had no inkling of the devious machinations of the Society for Understanding between Peoples and could not know the political significance of the murder of a horse like Man o' War, whose picture hangs in Kentucky distilleries and state offices like those of the President. I happened to find this out from a student of German literature from Lexington, Kentucky, whom the Count brought along to the bar one evening.

When I had to empty Ida's apartment of everything she had assembled during her life, I found three boxes full of dolls in folk costume that Ida had reserved to give to her own friends. I gave them to the children playing next to the rubbish bins where I threw Ida's lingerie, old shoes, and miscellaneous useless legacy before Ida herself was turned to ashes.

*

I no longer wanted to work for Beerenbaum,

although upon closer examination I could be no more guilty than a typewriter. Who would pronounce a typewriter guilty simply because a murderer had typed his confession on it? But I was not a typewriter, even if my behavior with Beerenbaum would suggest that I could be used like one: I was dependable, prompt, service-free - in short, quality German labor. In the meantime (I was the only one to perceive it) something began to spread inside me, an amorphous growth that coiled through my veins like bindweed, rankled around my heart, and constricted my stomach so much that I was sometimes afraid there was no room left in my chest cavity to breath.

My outburst proved that I lacked the mental distance of a natural scientist who can impassively watch a lion tear apart a zebra - how it stalks its prey, where it bites first, whether it kills quickly or slowly. He considers it natural for a lion to tear a zebra to pieces, something not subject to a moral value judgment. Had I been able to observe Beerenbaum scientifically or, better still, with the inanimate eye of a camera, I would no more have been able to feel I was his victim than the naturalist feels a victim of the lion. The naturalist doesn't hate the lion. I hated Beerenbaum.

I hated him when his legs, recalling his

earlier self-assured appearances, simulated his youthful gait; I hated him when, in order to think, he demonstratively threw his head back, closing his eyes, and I was unable to stop looking at his outstretched neck where I could see his pharynx traced beneath his wrinkled skin; I remembered I had heard that to strangle someone quickly all you have to do is break the hyoid bone. I was repelled by the delicate, shrivelled skin on his powerful hands; I was irritated by a certain tone in his voice, a hypocritical gentleness that began the moment he talked to me outside the subject matter we had agreed upon. I even hated the frailty of his body, which he sought to hide with expensive cardigans and which, if there had been a clear explanation for my boundless revulsion, I should have rather liked. It was as if I instinctively hated Beerenbaum, as if there were a genetic code in me that warned me against Beerenbaum the way it warns a chicken against a goshawk. The chicken is afraid of the goshawk, but doesn't hate it. I asked myself what it is in humans that turns fear into hate. I would not have had to hate Beerenbaum if I weren't afraid of him.

Later, when I saw Beerenbaum in his crib deathbed helpless before another power, against which Beerenbaum's power during his lifetime looked like a light bulb against the sun, I could have made peace with him. He was beaten, not by me, but I could have felt like the victor during these minutes. Then, grasping and brazen, Beerenbaum extended his deathly white hand toward me. I had to fear Beerenbaum even as he was dying, and he was beaten only when he was dead.

The evening after Sensmann's visit I resolved never to set foot in the house at Silent Close No. 6 again. I no longer wished to work for Beerenbaum. I wanted to learn to play the piano.

*

Thekla Fleischer let out a brief cry when she saw me standing in front of her door. "What a surprise," she said. Was she happy or frightened to see me? She led me into the room next to the balcony; there was a bright tea-warmer on the oval table. The white light of a streetlamp shone through the window. "Excuse me," Thekla Fleischer said, and switched on the floor lamp, "I was just dreaming a bit." She placed a second cup on the table, offered me a chair, and sat down on the sofa where she had apparently spent half the evening dreaming in the dark. Her eyes behind her thick glasses were a bit moister than usual. Maybe she had been crying, for joy or misery. She ran her hand through her hair as if she wanted to fix the knot she had long sacrificed to her love; her hands couldn't get used to the change, picking distractedly in her dandelion hairdo.

"No one ever visits me," she said. "Except for my students, nobody visits me. When my mother was still alive her girlfriends came to visit us, but they've died by now too." She ran her hand across the embroidered tablecloth and smiled as though she had to excuse herself to me for being lonely.

"It's so nice of you to pay me a visit," she said, balancing the "so" on the tip of the sentence with her high voice.

"Yes," I said, "we've been living in the same building for ten years and have yet to visit each other."

She looked at me expectantly, and I felt I was being urgently invited to explain what had moved me to knock at Thekla Fleischer's door on, of all days, this one. She supposed I had come as a guest, so it was impossible for me to say that I too wanted to become a student not a visitor, that really no one paid her a visit, not even me.

"I had quite a day today," I said. At least that wasn't a lie.

She sat quietly on the Biedermeier sofa. Her
dark-red satin outfit, a broad, softly pleated
tunic with equally broad knickerbockers, was
the same color as the small roses on the sofa
cover. I had never thought about what Thekla
Fleischer's apartment might look like. Now that
I had seen it, I couldn't imagine it being any
different. A delicate secretary bureau, the
dresser, the old brass floor lamp with a
yellowing silk shade, the huge myrtle in front of
the window, a beautiful carpet worn where
steps led to the door, everything had something
of Thekla Fleischer's faded old-fashionedness,
old Thekla Fleischer in her flowing garments
that always looked a bit ridiculous when she
walked with her demure baroque hips along our
narrow street jammed with parked cars.

"These are all heirlooms," she said, "I've
known them as long as I can remember. I'm so
lucky Mama never threw anything away, when
you think of all the ugly junk there is to buy. I
need to be surrounded by beautiful things."

I thought of my black chairs and said it all
goes well together, her and the furniture. She
looked pretty on the sofa, I added.

She clapped her hands like a little girl.
"Oh," she cried, "you're making a compliment.
Isn't it a marvellous day today. We have to
celebrate, I still have a liqueur Aunt Hildi sent

me for my birthday. May I offer you some?"

Without waiting for an answer, she ran off into the kitchen and came back with two liqueur glasses and an unopened bottle.

"It's Italian," she said, and spelled the name: "Amaretto."

It was pretty sweet; we both liked it. Thekla Fleischer told me that she had been living in this apartment since her parents moved with her from Güstrow to Berlin forty years ago; first there were three, her father, her mother, and herself, then two after her father died, and now she was alone. Her mother had also given piano lessons. "That's how things go on, isn't it?"

I said I had the impression that we were condemned in this life to make the same mistakes over and over again. Even if we were radically to change our outward circumstances in the belief that we could prevent a certain conflict from ever happening again, somewhere or other the same trap was waiting to catch us without fail.

"But Miss Polkowski," she emphatically placed her empty glass on the table, "you mustn't say that. You are such a strong person. Like Mama. Mama was also a strong person. I've been told you quit your good job although you have to fend for yourself. If I had your courage, dear me, I'd have chopped my piano to bits and thrown the pieces out the window long ago."

She sat on the rose-pattern sofa, her head tilted slightly backward, so the curve of her round chin and her neck stood out defiantly, her gaze directed aimlessly over the myrtle and out the window.

I asked whether she liked playing the piano. It was my dream, a dream that never came true, to be able to play the piano, because my parents gave me an accordion for my birthday instead of a piano, for pedagogical reasons. I first had to prove that I seriously loved music before they would disfigure their cramped apartment with a black beast. But how could I prove my love for music on an accordion?

She didn't listen to me. She was still looking out the window she wanted to throw her piano through.

"I'd like to be a terrorist," she said all of a sudden; "terrorists are never alone. Not when they throw bombs, and later in prison everyone gets excited if they have to serve their sentences in solitary. I sit here by myself every day and no one gets excited about that." She put her feet on the sofa and drank the liqueur in a single draught. "Yes," she said, "I'm that far gone. Isn't that terrible? Mama would turn in her grave if she knew I said such horrible things. Mama was against all forms of violence. A strong person like Mama can afford to be against all forms of violence. Of course, I refuse to kill people, but I also refuse to be alone all the time and not to see anyone except lazy, untalented piano students."

The tiny tea-warmer flame was reflected in her thick glasses, lending her a touch of foolhardiness. If it hadn't been for those heavy hips I really could have imagined her as a terrorist, an old-fashioned Russian anarchist in a waisted travelling dress and laced boots, a tyrannicide who looks her victim mercilessly in the eye while aiming at his forehead.

"You seemed to be so happy of late," I said.

If I wasn't able to ask her whether I could be her student, I at least wanted to find out what had brought about Thekla Fleischer's peculiar transformation. I could no longer detect the irritating gaiety I had seen in her during the previous weeks. Instead there was a helpless rebellion, longing for a forbidden act; I knew only too well not to fall immediately under its spell. But what had happened to Thekla Fleischer's love, perhaps the only one in her life, to which she had sacrificed her long hair, for which she had bared what she had chastely hidden for decades?

"Ah, Miss Polkowski," she said, and her high voice fluttered like a captive bird, "if you only knew. I can't help crying again."

She saved herself with nervous laughter. "Shall I show you something really beautiful?" she asked, finally showing the silly smile I hadn't seen during the last few hours. She picked up the sofa pillow, which covered a black-and-white photo, a man's portrait. Thekla Fleischer's secret. She carefully took the photo by its edges between her thumb and middle finger so as not to leave prints on the glossy surface and placed it in the palm of my hand. The man in the picture was sixty, perhaps seventy years old and looked like the actor Curt Götz. The outer corners of his eyes were curved slightly downward; strands of white hair fell on his forehead; narrow, finely molded lips; a face without a trace of disgust. No man like Beerenbaum, more like one of the few sympathetic old men, a former rebel, a sleepwalker who could be tamed only by approaching death.

Six months ago, this man, she told me, had come to her door unannounced, holding his seven-year-old grandson by the hand, to ask whether she would teach the boy to play the piano. He brought him to the lesson three times, sat quietly on the sofa, listened and looked at her steadily, so much so that she became nervous. After the third lesson, quite against his nature, he rushed the boy to leave, making him forget his music, so that the grandfather had to come back to fetch it half an hour later. They drank tea together and talked about music. He, Thekla Fleischer said, loved Schubert. He was an artist who had met the painter Kurt Schwitters when he was young. During this hour together he had told her things so indecent she dared not repeat them, no, things so wonderful that no one should say such things about themselves, not even quoting someone else. Since that day they met regularly. The misfortune that finally did fill Thekla Fleischer's eyes with tears was simply that the man Thekla Fleischer called HE - was married, and that his daughter, the boy's mother, lived on our street, in the building opposite ours.

"I don't know whether I'm happy or unhappy," she said, and pressed her face into her large, powerful pianist's hands. She crouched in her broad dark-red satin outfit in the corner of the rose-pattern sofa, her tousled grey hair fused with the light from the floor lamp to a glowing halo around her head.

I poured us some more Amaretto and said I didn't see what was so unhappy about her story. To love is always a blessing, even unrequited love is a blessing, less than requited love, but also a blessing.

I was thinking of Beerenbaum, whom I hated.

"Do you know what a misfortune is?" I said. "A misfortune is when you can't stand to look at a certain person's neck without thinking you want to break the hyoid bone in his throat. When an unknown fear turns into hate and runs through your dreams like a poisonous trail of phlegm, when you realize you can become a murderer and you aren't terrified by the thought. *That* is misfortune."

My voice was emphatic. She gave me such a frightened look that I stopped talking. Then I found I had already said too much not to continue. I told her about Beerenbaum, how I had met him in the café, that he wore the same cardigan and the same Bordeaux-red leather slippers as my father, that Beerenbaum was writing his memoirs and that I refused to let him use my brain.

"Initially, I simply didn't like him; as time passed I found I hated him. I have to think about him, although I do not want to think about him. I dream about him. Before entering his house my heart beats the way it does for someone I love. I gloat when he looks bad, and it occurs to me he could suddenly die of a heart attack while I am standing next to him. He hasn't done anything to me. He pays me five hundred marks a month. It is him I hate, but what do I hate so much?"

"Forget what you hate and go after what you love," she whispered to herself. "That's what Mama always used to say. Mama was a strong person. I shouldn't hate the piano; if it weren't for the piano he wouldn't have come, now would he?"

She hadn't heard of Beerenbaum or the Hotel Lux. She said she didn't understand politics.

"What's there to understand?" I asked. "One day, sooner or later, you simply know that's the way things are. It's quite simple as long as you only ask what and don't ask why: all around you there's something lying on the streets called power. In sandboxes, bars, offices, streetcars, in beds, it's everywhere. Everyone takes a little of it and some can't get enough - so they become policemen, porters, or politicians. There's nothing more to understand.

"The worst part of it is when the same power and same rules apply in your own home as outside. My father ruled over my school and he ruled at home. He even determined when I was allowed to enter the bathroom in the morning. I couldn't take him to court; there was no one to contradict him. Here, in your place,"

I said with a glance taking in the lamp, the sofa, and the other furniture, lingering on the piano, "he would have had no say."

"Mama wouldn't have allowed that," she said.

We split the rest of the Amaretto, told each other our first names, that we were going to use familiar forms of address from now on, and we kissed each other on the mouth. Our mouths were sticky from the liqueur. I promised to visit her again soon. I said nothing about playing the piano.

We celebrated Thekla Fleischer's wedding in January. In the country. There was snow on the ground.

*

The double chin sat down in his chair in the first row. The violinists clasped their instruments between their chins and shoulders, looked each other dully in the eyes, and the first violinist nodded. This time it was Mozart's *Ave verum corpus*. In front of the coffin lay the wreaths and garlands, with large wreaths in the center almost as large as tractor tires, covered with flowers for strewing, primroses and forget-me-nots. I was fascinated. The harmonium player was at least two tones off, and distracted me from finding out who had donated this monument to bad taste. The yellow and light-blue flowers for strewing looked like a thread-bare covering for the huge wheel: the wolf's snout beneath Little Red Riding Hood's grand-mother's pretty lace bonnet. I was standing too far away to decipher the gold inscription on the yellow, carefully draped ribbon. The question was whether the wreath was meant as a symbol for the dead, whether its huge dimensions were supposed to recall how important the deceased was and the graceful flowers his delicate soul; or whether they were meant to represent the bearer. Although the primroses and forget-me-nots seemed to suggest a female donor, I quickly discarded this idea. Women wouldn't have been able to carry the thing. It must have been a financially strong institution consisting mostly of men: a ministry, the police, the army, or the Party. There were twelve wreaths lying around Beerenbaum's coffin; nine with red, two very small ones with white sashes of artificial silk honoring the deceased, and that puzzling monster with the prominent apolitical ribbon.

Who dared deny Beerenbaum the color red in parting? On the left, where the heart lies, red like blood. I had seen Beerenbaum's blood. It had suddenly flowed out of his right nostril - three heavy, bright-red drops fell on the white paper in front of him before he managed to take a handkerchief out of his pocket and press it against his nose. I had asked for the first time about the Hotel Lux. Whether they had known, whether he had known. The desk lamp was on, casting a harsh cross-light on Beerenbaum's face.

"What?" he asked. He knew what I had asked him about. Still he asked, as if he could avoid the answer with this verbal reflex.

"That," I said.

"No one knew anything." He looked at me. He wanted me to believe him.

"Did you suspect?"

He clenched his left hand into a fist. "We were fighting against Hitler." He drew out the syllables, accompanying each one with a painfully slow, impatient, imploring, final blow by his fist on the table top.

"And once Hitler had been defeated?"

"We built a state. Learned, learned, and learned again."

"Didn't you miss the comrades you lived next door to in the Hotel Lux?"

He tried to take a deep breath. His lips trembled, his face turned deep red. Then blood flowed out of his right nostril, ran down the wrinkled delta of his upper lip and dripped onto the empty sheet of paper before him.

I felt disgust. Not at Beerenbaum's blood. I

didn't feel sick at the sight of blood, not even my own. (I felt sick at the sticky sweetness of my own blood only when I had injured myself and had to lick the blood from my finger to keep it from soiling the carpet or my clothes.) It wasn't Beerenbaum's blood that disgusted me as it spread along the barely visible stubble on his skin; no, it was the fact that instead of an answer, he provided me with his old pill-polluted blood artificially diluted against thrombosis, the fact that through this cheap trick he had turned himself into a victim to forbid me from asking questions. He finally found a handkerchief.

"Didn't you wish to know what had happened to your comrades after they dragged them out of bed in the Hotel Lux?"

I couldn't stop. His face was covered by the handkerchief. I could see only his eyes, which were either imploring or filled with hate. Why did I feel no pity? "Weren't you afraid they would come one day to take you away? Or your wife? Like they took away the wife of Erich Mühsam and Alice Abramowitz, who was sent to Siberia to chop wood, survived, and returned a cripple. Have you seen your comrade Alice Abramowitz since then?"

He didn't answer; he pressed the handkerchief against his nose and mouth. The desk lamp was now blinding him; he turned the shade toward the wall with his sick, trembling hand.

"What did you say to her? Did you say to her what even her son said to her when he was allowed to see her again after fifteen years? He did not say a word because he believed what he had been told in the children's home - that his mother was a Nazi spy."

Like a sated bloodsucker I didn't let go of Beerenbaum until the handkerchief was drenched in his blood. I knew how I looked now, as if someone had held a mirror in front of my face - my mouth twisted, my jaw and neck tense, my eyes narrowed. The last sentences sounded rude and mean to me, and yet it was my voice.

"Can I help you?" I asked after a while.

He shook his head.

I left him four paper tissues I found in my handbag.

What color would Beerenbaum's blood be now as he lay pale as wax dressed in his dove-grey suit between silk cushions and words could no longer mortally wound him. It wasn't the red blood of the living.

The first sentence he dictated the following Friday was: "My wife was arrested during the autumn of 1939."

My fingers were so stiff I couldn't write. He looked at me like someone who was taking aim before making a throw.

"She was taken to Ravensbrück concentration camp."

Excited, out of breath, he stood up, went to the door and turned toward me - "That's not in Siberia," he screamed, and left the room.

I stared where he had just been sitting. Behind the window there was a timeless light, the bare branches of the copper beech were motionless, everything about me was quiet as if I were held prisoner in a photograph. You are always right, I thought, whatever I say to you; those with a biography have a monopoly on misfortune. As soon as I open my trap to mention mine, they shove a tough nut like Ravensbrück or Buchenwald down my throat. Eat it or die. He had taken from Tuesday to Friday to prepare this one minute, these three sentences; he had imagined how I would have to sit with stiff fingers, speechless for shame, unable to repeat my question about the Hotel Lux because I had nothing to show in my life that entitled me to ask such a question.

I wrote: "Grete was arrested in the autumn of 1939. They put her in Ravensbrück concentration camp. Siberia is located near Ravensbrück."

*

The violinists placed their instruments in their cases but did not close them. The man on the harmonium played "The International" like the "The Party's Over." A short man carried a black satin cushion with Beerenbaum's medals in the palms of his hands through the cordon, followed by four men, the coffin containing the dead Beerenbaum on their shoulders. Behind the coffin came the large wreaths, each carried by two men. The small wreaths and bouquets were picked up by their donors, who carried them in the funeral procession. I waited for the wreath with the flowers for strewing. As two men in uniform carried them past me, I was able to read "A final salute from the soldiers on the invisible front" on the half of the ribbon hanging on my side.

Of course, a colossal funeral wreath disguised as a summer meadow, the Stasi secret police, who else? It was only now that I recognized Michael Beerenbaum - he was one of the wreath-bearers. I saw him for the first time in uniform.

The seated violinists were ready to jump, their instruments lying vertically on their thighs like crutches they would prop themselves on as soon as the assembly left the chapel. They pushed the mourners through the doors with their eyes.

I was last. Two of them nodded good-bye to me when I smiled at them.

The path from the chapel to the rectangle of earth that had been dug for Beerenbaum in a special section of the cemetery began across the main path toward the exit. I followed at about ten to fifteen feet from the procession. No one would have noticed if I had left the path and walked between the graves, placed my freesia on some forgotten grave, and left the cemetery through a side entrance.

I could have gone home now. In half an hour at most Beerenbaum would be lying in his plot, under the still loose earth; for a few days the pile of wreaths would betray the newcomer, until Michael Beerenbaum's wife or a cemetery attendant he had paid transformed the fresh mound into an ordinary grave with ice ferns and conifers. Still, I continued walking behind the others. I hadn't seen enough yet.

*

Beerenbaum called me three days after Sensmann's visit. He said unfortunately he had to cancel tomorrow's, Tuesday's, session owing to an urgent appointment with his doctor, and that we couldn't continue work until Friday.

Beerenbaum was the slyest old man I knew. He guessed I was determined not to return to his house. He wanted to keep me. It was precisely my open anger against him and everything he stood for that seemed to bring him to life, as if he dictated his sentences against me only to prove to me that my anger wasn't worth a damn, that it couldn't hurt him, that I was even serving him with my hate.

His call surprised me. I had planned to call him the next day at exactly three in the afternoon to inform him, as unemotionally as possible, that I regarded my employment with him as terminated, immediately, and to hang up, without giving him a chance to answer.

I looked for the sentence I had prepared for him; I couldn't remember it. It would have been easy to say: I won't be coming on Friday either, or, I'm not coming at all, or simply - No. Say no and hang up. That would have been a possibility.

I allowed him to end the conversation quickly by claiming he was in a hurry. Had we talked longer I may have decided not to go, but his final, unchallenged "Until Friday" meant our work relationship would continue as if it had never been in doubt.

This was one possible explanation. There were others. My struggle against Beerenbaum was no longer a struggle against him alone; that was clear from when I set the coffee table for Victor Sensmann. If I had simply wanted to put an end to his power over me, I would have stuck to my resolution not to enter his house again. But I had by now reached the stage of enmity that makes you miss the object of your hatred.

Shortly after three the following afternoon I phoned his house to see if he had really gone to the doctor's. He picked up the phone after the fourth ring; he said "hello" three times before I hung up.

*

Beerenbaum placed two glasses and a bottle of brandy on the table. To make up, he said, and sat down across from me. The Rheinmetall typewriter stood between us. He asked me to open the bottle. I filled the glasses halfway.

"Don't be so half-hearted," Beerenbaum said, "or we'll only have half a reconciliation." "Miss Polkowski," he said, "or may I call you Rosalind, or better still, Rosa, like our Rosa, like our Rosa Luxemburg?"

I didn't know how to say no, so I said it was

all right.

"I've been thinking a lot about you over the past few days, Rosa. You are an intelligent, attractive woman in the prime of life. I don't know about your life, except for your strange maxim that you do not wish to think in return for money. When you recently left this house all excited, I asked myself: Why is she so bitter? I know you do not wish to talk to me about this. But look, I'm a curious old man and I would like to understand what gets you so worked up against me. To be honest, I feel I am being treated unjustly."

He held his salientia face toward me and waited for an answer. I looked at the window, the door, like a child who doesn't know an answer standing in front of her teacher. To gain time, I drank some cognac. I have to be like the naturalist, I thought, crawl through all the mire, have my flesh torn by pointed rocks, lie calmly in hot sand for days on end without feeling like I was a victim of the lion. I wasn't supposed to say: People like you have ruined my life. I had to lure him, to seduce him to talk about himself instead of me. He was not sitting behind his desk; I wasn't taking notes. I had to say something which he couldn't answer with the legend of his life, a legend he too believed by now; something outside of politics.

"Discussions in which men try to convince each other of their own importance drive me crazy," I said.

He laughed, revealing his teeth, embedded so tightly and evenly in his artificial gums that I could see them before me floating in a pungent denture cleanser.

"You wouldn't happen to hate men as well?" he asked.

"Why, as well?"

It took him a few seconds to understand what I had asked.

"No, no," he said, "it's just an idiotic figure of speech. You're no enemy in my eyes, Rosa, quite the contrary. Sometimes you even remind me of my wife Grete. I have seen enough enemies in my life to know you aren't one of them."

For the first time I saw that he drank alcohol. The way he raised the glass to his lips - outstretched elbow, rigid wrist - was not the way a social drinker drank. Either he had acquired the habit as a young man and retained it, or he now drank more than I had assumed. He emptied the liquor into his mouth and let it flow over his tongue into his esophagus, without swallowing. I would like to have known how he could tell I wasn't an enemy, but I didn't ask because I presumed he wanted to provoke precisely this question.

"Did Grete hate men too?" I asked.

He leaned back his head, though he did not close his eyes, as if thinking, letting them wander along the ceiling as if he could read there what he wanted to say to me. "Grete" - he pronounced her name devotedly, like that of a saint - "Oh, yes, Grete could hate passionately, just as she could love. She unrelentingly hated her enemies, men such as Krupp, Scheidemann, Hindenburg, Hitler - and their wives . . . But," Beerenbaum continued, now looking at me, "she loved her comrades Thälmann, Dimitroff, Pieck, and her comrade Herbert Beerenbaum, because she was a Communist. My comrade, a whole life long."

Beerenbaum inclined his head to one side, closed his eyes, concentrated as if listening carefully to a very gentle voice, raised his hand to his chest, and declaimed, rolling his *r*'s:

> *Our country lay in blackest night,*
> *You captive and mistreated,*
> *I, banished to lands faraway,*
> *Our glances both directed:*
> *Far off the scarlet banner waved.*
> *Thank you, Comrade Grete.*
>
> *Down, disheartened, near despair,*
> *Sacred Moscow close to flames:*

I thought of your fair golden hair
And your heart that knows no qualms.
Your stout spirit
My weakness all abated.
Thank you, Comrade Grete.

He lowered his hand, with which he had accompanied the verses in broad rhythmic gestures and said, his eyes still half closed: "Yes, I wrote that for her. I know I am no poet, but these words of thanks expressed themselves in verse. You are too young to know what it means to be sure of an upright person during barbaric times. Pour us another drink, Rosa, that one will only half quench your thirst. Grete and I were not yet married when the Party decided to send me abroad for the duration. Grete remained in Germany. Before I left we promised each other that should we both survive the Nazis, we would meet after the war on Sunday at nine-thirty in front of the Friedrichstadtpalast. Grete began going there six weeks before me. She came every Sunday; on the sixth Sunday I too came with a big bouquet of daisies I had stolen from the garden of a bombed-out villa. Daisies were Grete's favorite flowers."

He downed the second cognac as resolutely as the first. Although I thought the poem was horrible, I couldn't help believing him for the first time. I saw him before me, a young man or almost young man, with open collar and shirt sleeves, the daisies in his hand walking through the mountains of rubble in central Berlin. I smelled the chalky dust rising from the ruins mixing with the summer morning air and the smell of war. I saw a young woman, driven by hope and oppressed by disappointment, crossing the Spree Bridge; how they ran to each other and could not believe they were back together again. All the pictures I had seen in real life and films became this single picture.

"Didn't your comrades tell you that Grete was alive and in the city?" I asked.

"I arrived in Berlin on Saturday and slept with a comrade from Pankow who had heard from Grete but did not know where she lived. It's exactly as I told you. Grete was thirty-three and I was forty. Believe me, I wept when I saw the city again. Everywhere I looked there was nothing but destruction - destroyed buildings, destroyed people, every other person a Nazi, and the rest fellow-travelers. And we, a handful of half-starved, defeated Communists and anti-fascists had to put things straight. Arising from the ruins and turned toward the future, yes, that's how it was."

Then, as during my first visit to Beerenbaum's house, I was seized by the illusion that made me believe I had heard this all before, that I knew every sentence that would follow what had just been said, including the tone of voice it would be uttered in. I had heard the exact same things before, everything.

"They were good times, but hard times," I said, because I knew this sentence had to be uttered at this point.

"Yes," Beerenbaum said, "they were hard times, but good ones. We achieved a great deal."

"And you will defend that against anyone who..."

"...wishes to turn back the clock. Yes, indeed, we will," Beerenbaum said. Then he looked at me in astonishment. "I had no idea we agreed on this so completely."

"I was just quoting my father," I said.

"Is your father a Communist?"

"He was a school principal. He's dead now."

Beerenbaum sighed as he attempted to open the bottle himself this time. His right hand trembled like an addict just before he collapses, but somehow he managed. There was a brief hint of pain or fear on his face, as if I had just spoken of his own, perhaps imminent, death, not that of my father. I sometimes asked myself what it would be like when they were all dead and Thekla, Bruno, and I would be old - what we would defend and what we would pass off as advancing the clock. I was forty-two and had accomplished nothing worth defending. I also believed Bruno had nothing to show for his life. Bruno would probably have said he was defending the rights of the Latins against the steadily increasing hordes of the non-Latins: Lawrence Sterne against Peter Hacks, Schopenhauer against Lukacs, *Don Giovanni* against *West Side Story*, which in the end meant that Bruno was doing exactly as I was - defending himself. I had nothing to defend except myself, while Beerenbaum regarded the whole clockwork of history as his doing which had to be defended by force of arms, if necessary, like my father often used to say, and Beerenbaum presumably would also say. This minute I understood that everything depended on Beerenbaum's death, his death and that of his generation. Not until what they had done was no longer sacred, until the only criteria for retaining or dropping something was its utility would I be able to find out what I would like to have done with my life. And then it would be too late. Sometimes I thought up sentences I had never thought. They rose from mysterious depths somewhere in my liver, spleen, or elsewhere in my entrails, where they rumbled at night while I was dreaming. Very rarely and unexpectedly they sent sentences to my consciousness like messages in a bottle.

All of these sentences began with "the day after tomorrow." The day after tomorrow the desert will be covered with ice. The day after tomorrow the cockroaches will usher in the kingdom of heaven. The day after tomorrow water will fall into the sky - non-swimmers beware. They never began with "tomorrow." "Tomorrow" wasn't my day yet. What would happen tomorrow was already written down in Beerenbaum's appointment book. The day after tomorrow was the day following Beerenbaum's death.

We sat opposite each another like two people drinking in a bar. His eyes were already glazed. The alcohol slowly aroused the hopeful impulse to tell things we are all born with, but which most of us have lost by the time we die.

I imagined myself explaining to him - carefully, trying not to hurt him - why existing conditions he also had a part in creating compelled me to wish his death. I would be happy, I would say, if I were able to feel indifferent, even sad, at your death. Don't think I'm not moved by your love for Grete that survived twelve years of waiting. Or that I can't feel the fear that must have tormented you night after night in the Hotel Lux. I even wish I were able to be proud of you, you who resisted, who weren't a Nazi or a cowardly yes-man. Still, I would say that I had to wish your death because you have stolen every house, every piece of paper, every street, every thought, everything I need to live, and won't give them back. You force me to do the most abominable thing I can imagine - to wish someone's death. How could I want you to go on living? Then I would ask him: Do you understand me?

I didn't expect him to agree to die. I simply wanted him to understand that given the state of things I had to wish this. I could not imagine his answering: Yes, I understand you. He would have had to understand all sorts of things to answer yes. I was ten years old. My parents had gone to Thuringia on vacation. I stayed in Berlin with Ida. My parents needed to recover from the hard work they did all year long in the school, Ida said. If I went along I would only bother them. I hadn't met my father until three years earlier. One morning he walked into the kitchen - my bed was in the corner behind the door - took me in his arms, and my mother said, "This is your daddy." I wanted to have a father. Everyone had a mother. But if you could say, "My father said I couldn't do that," that was something very precious. Ida, who had lived with us until then, moved out, and my father moved in. My mother had taken a crash course to qualify as a trainee teacher, and my father, who must have forgotten his own dreams during the war and prisoner-of-war camp, did the same. During the summer when I was ten and my parents went to Thuringia for rest and relaxation, I had known my father three years and had not yet addressed him with a word indicating our parent-child relationship. I had never called him father, daddy, or papa, though I would have liked nothing better. I was simply waiting for a little sign of his approval so I wouldn't be exposed as a liar (to him and to me) the moment I uttered the word.

This summer I let Ida show me how to make lemon cream. Lemon cream was my father's favorite dessert; it elicited unequivocal praise from him every time Ida brought it to him in a small glass bowl. Every evening I mixed egg whites, sugar, cream, and lemon juice until the cream was finally stiff, so that mine was identical to Ida's much-praised lemon dessert. To welcome my parents back from their vacation in Thuringia, I used twenty eggs to make the biggest bowl of lemon cream my father had ever seen in his life, and I imagined his eating it all up by himself with a big spoon, with an occasional thankful glance meant for me and me alone.

He shoveled down half of the bowl of lemon cream before my very eyes. "Rosi made it," Ida said softly. Being an unmarried sister-in-law, she felt merely tolerated in our house, living in constant fear my father would consider her a bother. Perhaps he didn't hear Ida's remark about my having made the lemon cream, perhaps he wasn't interested. Who knows what happens to men during wars. It seemed normal to my father that there was a sufficient amount of his favorite dessert on the table and that he didn't have to thank anyone for it. He gobbled and gobbled. They sent me to bed early.

"You have a strange way of reasoning, Rosa," Beerenbaum said. "I ask you whether your father was a Communist, and you answer he was a school director and is dead. Was he a Communist?"

"That was the way he saw it."

"And you?"

"I don't know what a Communist is."

"A Communist is someone who fights for Communism. And, as Brecht said, Communism is the simple thing that is hard to realize," Beerenbaum said. "You wish to provoke me, Rosa. Of course, as a historian you know all of this."

I said that a Communist is someone who doesn't thank a child who gives him a big bowl of lemon cream because he happens to be busy with world revolution. This dilemma determines a Communist's life from beginning to end and I was afraid Communists would rather let the world be blown up than permit it not to be Communist, precisely because for Communists there is nothing more important than Communism. They go so far that every awful thing they do is called Communist because they can't stand something not being Communist. My father probably would have called his relationship to lemon cream and me Communist simply because he couldn't imagine anything else. I could tell that Beerenbaum couldn't follow my alcohol-inspired logic.

"Lemon cream. What does lemon cream have to do with Communism?" He shook his head, annoyed. Obviously my relationship with my father was difficult, he said, and I'd ended up making a perfect muddle of private and social spheres - hardly the result of a scientific point of view.

I said that I was an empiricist. Empiricists are the only ones able to become smarter with the years because experience is the only thing that increases with age, while everything else, including the ability to think logically and scientifically, decreases with age, as a result of defective nerve endings and faulty connections in the brain, meaning that it can't be avoided through training and good will. I had decided to base my world view entirely on experience so that it wouldn't collapse when I grew old. And experience had taught me that Communism and lemon cream do in fact have something to do with one another the moment you meet a Communist who likes lemon cream. If a lemon cream gobbler is a Communist, the child he doesn't thank will always connect the two. And someone who meets a Communist murderer knows for the rest of his life that Communism is also murderous.

Beerenbaum's frontal veins swelled blue. I wasn't sure whether I had stated my theory in a sober state, but at that moment it seemed to me to be perfect.

"Communism," I said after I had poured him and then myself another glass of brandy, "Communism cannot be better than Communists, no better than Herbert Beerenbaum and Fritz Polkowski."

Beerenbaum stared at his brandy glass, but did not touch it. "Miss Polkowski," he said, he had stopped saying Rosa, now it was Miss Polkowski. He asked himself where I, a university graduate, had left my reason. He was not able to attend a technical institute or university. He was self-taught, but the whole is more than the sum of its parts, that much he knew. He wanted to make up with me, he still wished to, but he would not permit me to heap scorn on the ideal to which he had devoted his life.

He loudly swallowed his saliva, either because he was excited or badly needed a drink.

I asked whether he really believed that generations of people would be born in order for Communists to test their ideals on them. I said my ideal was to be a cat, because they aren't subject to Communists or anyone else.

"Rosa," he said - so it was Rosa again - "have you ever asked yourself what you would have been under the Nazis?"

"Perhaps I would have been a Communist," I said.

*

Beerenbaum's mourners moved with short steps past the uniform gravestones on either side of the path. Under each stone was a predecessor, a deceased, each of whom the cemetery regulations condemn to be remembered in prescribed inscriptions on granite blocks of the same dimensions. Deathly silence, graveyard silence. In the distance, the screeching of buses stopping and starting. I used to walk through cemeteries as in a fairy tale; I trusted this place concealing the darkest of secrets. An infinite number of stories all beginning with once upon a time. Here they all lay, uncomplaining, one layer on top of the other. They were permitted to stay on the earth to commemorate their life until the next generation of the dead pushed them even further into the depths. My own death was too far not to be tempted to lure it: come, show yourself, play with me. With the triumphal pose of someone whose life has just begun, I took it for a walk among the dead, whom I, the victor, showed that it was now my turn to live. Here, in a refuge of defenseless silence, I had confirmed that to which the world of living adults is not entitled. Here I secretly buried my parents, aunts, uncles, teachers and made sure of the time that would be my own. I now felt closer to those under the ground than the unsuspecting people, who like myself had been wandering among them twenty years ago.

Beerenbaum died three days after I visited him in the hospital. I found out about it from the newspaper.

*

My last image of Beerenbaum: his open, toothless mouth containing a dirty tongue that looked as if it was covered with mold; the irises of his eyes were wan and opaque, two tiny round windows into Beerenbaum's head. Then Beerenbaum's hand - like a white-skinned lizard - shot out from under the blanket and leaped at my chest with maw wide open. It was as if he had touched my bare heart. I later tried to believe he wanted to grab my arm or my shoulder - his hand missed its target only because he was too frail. But I couldn't forget the half-open, grinning mouth and the bright eyes in which his pupils had shrunk to tiny dots.

My father died aged sixty-three. He died at home in his bed at about one in the morning, alone. My mother's bedroom was next to my father's; the two rooms were linked by a door. He did not call for my mother during the night. He did not see death coming, or he had wished to remain alone with it. My father died sitting on the edge of his bed, smoking a cigarette. He must have been dead by the time the cigarette had burned to the end. The filter between his fingertips was ashes. He couldn't have felt it. My mother, who found him in the morning, thought he had fallen asleep sitting up. When she gently tried to wake him, he collapsed backwards with his stiff limbs onto the bed. And his dentures fell out of his mouth.

I think he knew he was dying. He had sat up,

lit a last cigarette, as smokers do - one more cigarette and then I'll leave. He hadn't switched on the floor lamp next to his bed. He no longer wanted to see, hear, or say anything, not even to my mother. He had not said anything for a long time. Sometimes when he was forced to say something, he would reluctantly move his face as if in pain. He taught school until the day he died. He found questions, even simple questions, agonizing. When I visited my parents, I actually visited only my mother; he retreated into the study, which was separated from the living room by a sliding door. The door was warped and hard to move. Each time my father underwent this exertion he twisted his face like an evil mask, as if he had saved up all of his hate and despair to discharge in this act. The inanimate existence of the door, which he knew could be overcome, must have been more than a bothersome obstacle. Or he would have called a carpenter. It seemed as if he wanted to educate the door, to clarify their relative strengths once and for all. During the last weeks before his death he was so weak he didn't so much as struggle against the door, protecting himself from our talk with loud pop music instead. He preferred listening to Mireille Matthieu. At the time I felt no pity for him. I was even gratified to watch him grow weaker. I asked myself, because I couldn't ask him, how he could stand in front of his pupils every day and talk about the history of class struggle. Every other year he had fresh new enemies. There are always a few who have to ask questions. What would my father answer if one of these brave souls wanted to know what happened in the Hotel Lux or in the Gulag Archipelago? Presumably he would ask where the questioner had gotten his information concerning these alleged events, where he had read about it, from whom he had heard about it, so that he could immediately defame the source of this base slander or malicious exaggeration and warn the pupil not to be the mouthpiece of enemy propaganda in the future. This was his successful defense against attack.

But the question remained. My father came home with it, he went to bed with it, he got up with it in the morning. What did my father do with all these questions? Did he simply forget them? Did he dismiss them as the provocation of blind young people? Did he secretly look for the answers, seduced by the unbelieving children whom he knew laughed at him and despised him because he did not want to give them the answers they themselves knew?

He should not have become a teacher. Had he remained a joiner, he would have been able to ask about things himself. He wouldn't have been afraid of tricky, forbidden questions. He detected a threat lurking behind every question meant to prove he was unfit - him, who used to be a worker - for his profession. His existence as a teacher was a thirty-year-long test he could fail every day. He most enjoyed reading encyclopedias. He learned them by heart, strictly by the alphabet, to make up for the education his origin, the war, and captivity had denied him. Instead of complete operas he listened to opera excerpts. He took no time for anything for fear he would stay what he was - a joiner with a primary school education.

From behind the window of his study framed by copper beeches, Beerenbaum let me ask him questions, himself discernible only as a silhouette. For this I was paid five hundred marks a month. Perhaps he wished to find out if he, the son of a working-class family from the Ruhr, self-taught, professor without a school-leaving diploma, would stand up to my questions. Questions he would never have tolerated in public.

Now that Beerenbaum is dead and I am walking behind his coffin as a witness to his burial, for the first time I feel pity for my father.

*

Monday afternoon I went to Alexanderplatz to ask at the music shop whether an Italian-German *Don Giovanni* libretto had arrived. I looked for the short-haired salesgirl I had bribed with twenty marks. She was standing, a pile of sheet music under her arm, in front of a shelf; she made a gesture with her free hand to wait and winked conspiratorially. She disappeared behind a curtain and came back with a light-green booklet. She removed a slip of paper fastened to it with a paper clip. "We finally managed to find it," she said, smiling contentedly like someone exhausted after finishing a hard job. I did not feel like giving her the praise she expected in addition to the twenty marks, but did so all the same. "I'd be lost without you," I said. The booklet cost one mark eighty-five pfennig. I said thank you, winked at her with one eye in the hope I could discover the secret of the recitatives to *Don Giovanni* and that I might consider translating other operas.

*

The bar was still empty. It smelled of floor polish. Simone was standing behind the bar, cleaning the taps.

"Heh, Rosi," she said.

I said: "Heh, Simone."

"A quick one?"

"Wine."

"A quick wine," Simone said and took an open bottle out of the refrigerator. I asked her about the American.

"He wrote," she said. "He wants to come." But when? She shrugged her shoulders and showed me her empty hands. Simone came from Mecklenburg, where Eberhard, known as Ebi, the bar owner, met her five years ago, where he had saved her from a life as a wreath-and-bouquet maker in a small town. They stayed together for three years. Then Ebi returned to his divorced wife and kept Simone to work in his bar.

"Never find an honest girl like her again," he said.

Simone met the American a year ago during Carnival. Since the summer he was back studying in Lansing, Michigan, where his family lived.

"He's already spoken to his parents," Simone said, "but all the paperwork, there's so much paperwork in America when you get married."

"America," I said.

"Uh huh, America," Simone said and threw

the rag into the sink. "But first I gotta get outa here, Rosi."

It really looked like she believed she was going to marry the American. She was Catholic and went to mass on Sunday. But, after all, if Ebi had brought her to Berlin, why shouldn't she be able to make it to Lansing, Michigan, with this American?

"Yeah, Rosi, if there's nothing you can do, you gotta wait," she said.

Then the skat players came, like every other Monday. Simone had no time for me now. I sat at the bar, drank my wine, and felt good.

When Bruno said the bar was the last preserve of male freedom, he meant that the bar was the preserve of freedom as such, because in German the only thing feminine about freedom is its grammatical gender, and it would never have occurred to Bruno to make such a statement. Bruno considered women the natural enemies of freedom and the telephone the most fearful device of repression in the hands of women. The question "Why didn't you call" could send him into deep depression when he came home at four in the morning with glazed eyes after a night out drinking. He would simply take off his coat and shoes, fall straight into bed, and say the telephone is a case for the Human Rights Commission and that he would write the UN first thing in the morning.

Both profane and mysterious, the bar was an anti-world, an Orcus in which other laws applied and urban natural right held sway. Whoever stepped into the realm of the bar was no longer under the power of the upper world but was subject to another order.

Kutte Kluge, retiree, former waiter, with the wide slant-eyed face of an Asian deity, sent at least five of those present into a state of nervous excitement the moment he entered the bar. They stopped talking and looked at him expectantly. Kutte Kluge was not only a bar celebrity like Bruno, he has a chess celebrity as well. With a cheap cheroot in the corner of his mouth, he stood in the door for a while as though he wanted to make sure the others noticed his appearance, while he searched for his worthiest opponent, nodded to him briefly without further ceremony, silently sat down at an empty table, where he was automatically brought a first beer and a chess board, and waited until the one he had chosen took his seat. Kutte Kluge beat Latins and non-Latins alike, men with degrees and without, everyone to whom he had served duck flambé and thanked for tips his entire life.

It seemed the bar brought a higher justice to life, and although I wasn't part of this, I still found it a consolation. Beerenbaum's power did not extend to the bar. He had as little say here as in Thekla Fleischer's apartment while her mother was still alive. If he wished to survive in the bar, he had to be able to argue with the Count about the isoglosses between the various spellings of the name Schmidt: Schmidt with *dt*, or Schmid with *d*, or Schmitt with *tt*, or even as Schmitz with *tz*. Or he had to be a good loser playing chess with Kutte Kluge, or, like Peti, be able to supply bath tubs and toilet bowls.

Luckily, Bruno wasn't completely sober when he finally arrived. He had probably taken a shortcut with a quick glass of beer at the sausage stand next to the Hotel Sofia on Friedrichstrasse. That beer did not make him drunk or even slightly high, but not quite as sober as if the dust of books and files still stuck to his tongue.

Bruno saw the light-green booklet lying in front of me on the bar, leaned back to increase the distance between us and proclaim his astonishment: "What's the matter with you, Rosa? I can't believe you're really interested in opera. Have you started climbing mountains and running around lakes, too?"

Bruno and I would probably have become a couple like Philemon and Baucis if I had been able to answer his question with a yes, without lying. But the thought of wearing myself out, of even placing myself in danger to climb some mountain peak, even a small one, was so far-fetched I suspected a psychic defect behind Bruno's passion for mountain-climbing. And as for running around a lake, which used to be one of Bruno's favorite Sunday pastimes before we met, I considered it to be both absurd and humiliating. As if one were eagerly to imitate the fate of Sisyphus - suffering hours of agony in order to arrive where you had started.

Once Bruno had secretly tried to take me around Lake Summt. After half an hour we were suddenly standing in a clearing with a free view of the lake. When I understood what Bruno was up to, I walked back in a huff along the same path we had come, though the other part of the path was shorter and, according to Bruno, more beautiful. I couldn't bring myself to do it.

"I'd like to be interested in opera," I said, "but I can't. It doesn't interest me."

"Rosa, I envy you," Bruno said. "One day when you're old and smart you'll be interested in opera. Then you can discover a whole world while I'll be bored because I already know everything."

Bruno always talked about the boredom waiting for him when he grew old whenever he found out that I didn't know all of the books by Dostoyevsky, Beckett, or Joyce. Then he would sigh and say, "Ah, I envy you, Rosa," while I was ashamed, because although Bruno and I were the same age, I had not read half as much as he had.

Bruno thumbed through the light-green booklet. Suddenly he raised an arm as if he were holding a baton in his hand, arched his stomach like a portly opera singer and sang:

> *E non voglio più servir*
> *E non voglio più servir.*

And I no longer wish to serve.

Then he let his arm fall to the bar and reach for his beer glass.

"What would you do if you no longer had to serve?" I asked.

" *Viva vita contemplativa*," Bruno called past me to the entire room, to where the Count was now sitting uncomfortably on the edge of a chair, waiting for Bruno to invite him to come over to us.

" *Viva vita contemplatissima*," the Count called out in return, jumping up so fast that he spilled half of his beer, and cut himself a path across to us. "Madame Rosalie," he kissed my hand. "Brünoh, I did not wish to disturb," the Count said, pointing out his tact.

"Rosa wants to know what we would do if

we no longer had to serve."

The Count sighed. "I tell you, Brünoh, you forget in the course of time. Sometimes I think I would continue to do what I do every day - look for words in dictionaries, in the course of a lifetime this becomes second nature. Then there's my age," the Count held a hand in front of his mouth to mute his voice, the hmtata. "You understand, Brünoh, excuse me, Madame Rosalie, it's dreadful." He cast a despairing glance upward. Bruno, who was fifteen years younger than the Count, laughed. I laughed too. "You laugh," the Count said. "I can scarcely dare to drink a beer anymore. Bad, bad, bad."

It looked as if he were about to cry. We swallowed the rest of our laughter with what we were drinking.

"What is your poet-retiree up to," Bruno asked.

"Do you know Herbert Beerenbaum?" I asked.

Bruno took one step backward. "Rosalind Polkowski," Bruno said, "you didn't want to tell me just now that the retiree whose right hand you replace is the villain, the archvillain Herbert Beerenbaum, the one they named "Professor" because he couldn't do his multiplication tables. Rosalind Polkowski with the Burgundian pride, who prefers smoking cheap cigarettes to leading an undignified life in an office like you and me, Count, as secretary to a torturer."

At this moment, because Bruno had mentioned him, both of us looked at the Count, who was standing between us with a pale face and apparently wanted to say something, but only moved his lips silently. Bruno forgot his tirade, set the Count up onto a barstool, and put his beer glass in his hand. The Count drew his hand across his dry eyes as though he wished to wipe away a tear.

"Pardon," he whispered, "a slight indisposition, but this name, Madame Rosalie - he reached for my hand - no, that of all people, you..."

He supported his head with both hands so that the strands of hair he had glued over his bald head from one ear to the other with pomade fell sideways, across one shoulder. Bruno and I were standing to either side of him, patted him on the shoulders, and said the sort of things one says when one wants to console someone but doesn't know about what.

"As if a ghost were haunting the room," the Count said. "The sudden mention of this name suffices to make me lose all bearing. For twenty-three years, Madame Rosalie, for twenty-three years."

Bruno ordered him a vodka, after which life

slowly returned to the Count's face and voice.

"I owe this man," the Count said, "whose name you will not hear from this mouth without a fecal expletive, which I would like to spare you, those three years, Brünoh, you know the years I mean."

"You've never talked about it," Bruno said.

The Count noticed the three thin strands of hair hanging on his shoulder, moistened his fingertips with beer, and stuck the hairs back firmly between his forehead and the back of his head. "Ah, Brünoh," he said, "you know that I'm a coward."

This is what had happened: In the spring of 1962, T., the assistant at the Faculty of East Asian Languages and Literatures, managed to escape to West Berlin via Prague. Shortly before that he had given the Count the manuscript of his doctoral dissertation on the pretext of the Count looking over the chapter on the Third Ming Dynasty. T. wrote the Count a coded letter from West Berlin requesting him to send him the manuscript. The Count went to Potsdam and sent the packet with an assumed return address. Both T. and the Count had forgotten that a third party, who just happened to be in the room at the time, knew about T. consigning the manuscript to the Count. Once it was clear that T. had fled, this third party reported the incident to Beerenbaum, who at the time held an ambiguous but highly influential position in the university administration. Beerenbaum called the Count into his office and requested him to hand over the manuscript he had mailed two weeks earlier from the main post office in Potsdam. The Count denied ever having seen the manuscript. Beerenbaum informed the Security Police. The Count was arrested the same day. He later found out that the opinion of the university which was read during the trial, calling the head assistant Karl-Heinz Baron a reactionary element hostile to the high goals of the new order, had been written by Beerenbaum himself and sent by university mail to the attention of the faculty director. The Count was sentenced to three years in prison.

"The informant died several years later in an auto accident," the Count said.

Suddenly, without actually being guilty, I was entangled in the Count's misfortune. I felt life had lured me into a devious trap, as if it wished to prove to me I couldn't get off that easily. It is a shame to think for money, to be sure. But what wouldn't be a shame? "After all, you also work at the same university, in the same department," I said to the Count.

"I was even happy they took me on again at

the time, which I owed completely to the intercession of a person with a bad reputation who, rightly, expected my presence to help him in his career in the field. I later had to provide this person with more than sixty per cent of his doctoral thesis. Do you remember, Brünoh? It would be unwise to accuse Madame Rosalie."

Bruno nodded, but did not look at me.

"We all live in a state of shame," I said, quoting one of Bruno's favorite sayings.

Bruno answered, "You too only learn what you want to learn, Rosa."

The evening did not take a happy turn. Bruno tried to convince me to stop working for Beerenbaum. I promised to give it some thought, although I knew I would keep my next appointment with Beerenbaum. I wanted to see the thing through to the end. I wanted to defeat Beerenbaum. I had taken him on as a lifelong task. I felt this more than I was conscious of it. I wanted to win a belated victory in my hopeless struggle against Beerenbaum.

"Why does one hate?" I asked Bruno. "What happens to me when I hate?"

"Do you hate, then?" I detected a hint of sympathy in his question, as if he had asked if I were sick.

"It seems like it."

"You hated when you were defeated."

"Or when you loved and weren't loved in return," I said.

"Then you were defeated," Bruno said.

"And you've never hated?"

"Well, all right," Bruno said, "I kind of made it up. How about you, Count?"

The Count pulled on his midnight-blue bow tie with the tiny silver stars. "I suppose it's a question of temperament. I despise, Bruno, I despise."

Bruno accompanied me to the tram stop. We were alone on the street. All that lay behind us was the echo of our own steps; TV sets flickered from a number of windows. I was freezing and every time that happened Bruno put his arm around my shoulders, and I envied him this gesture nature allowed him. Bruno would probably be freezing too if he hadn't known since he was a child that he would grow large, strong arms he had to put around every woman who walked next to him, freezing. But maybe Bruno was freezing too.

The driver raced the tram along the rails like a child playing rescue squad with his toy train. We lurched, screeched, and clattered through the sleeping, sparsely lit city. The streets looked strange so devoid of people. We also looked strange as the first persons who had come to this godforsaken place in which all the inhabitants had been either killed or driven out forty or fifty years ago by war or disease. Behind the building walls were skeletons in rotten beds, or they were sitting at tables or in front of television sets the instant they died. When we got off, we would have to walk over hordes of rats that had since conquered the city, millions of fat rats that had crawled out of the sewers into the open air when the dead had stopped throwing trash into the sewers. The tram driver was also a skeleton in uniform. He wasn't able to brake before he died and had been driving at this breakneck speed from the city center to Pankow and from Pankow to the city center. Only Bruno was alive. And me.

*

We celebrated Thekla Fleischer's wedding in January. "He wants it so much I can't say no," Thekla said to me, "although I know it is a sin. Mama would turn in her grave if she found out."

She looked at me through her thick eyeglasses as if I was supposed to know what she meant.

"She won't find out," I said.

"You think not?"

"She won't find out," I said again with the

certainty of an unbeliever, and thought that if the cosmea was right, Mama would now be a cat or a dog or an ant and judge moral matters differently from when she had been human.

Mr Solow had taken it into his head to marry Thekla Fleischer. But since he had been married thirty years and had nothing he could accuse Mrs Solow of except having known her too long, he ruled out divorce. Mrs Solow's real name was Mrs Wittig, because Solow was a stage name Theodor Wittig had assumed at the end of the 'forties, owing to an inspiration. For him Solow - the "w" was silent - meant the seal on the secret lone-wolfing he had decided to practise in light of the political catastrophe behind him and the one he saw coming. When required to show cause to the authorities for his pseudonym, he explained that he, Solow, or to be more exact, Vladimir Nikolaievich Solow - the "w" was pronounced - was a Soviet Communist he had met after the war, who shortly thereafter died of typhoid fever.

Mr Solow wished to marry Thekla without breaking the rules and regulations of common decency. He wished to marry her before God, although he did not believe in God. But he believed in something that was greater and more lasting than transient man, and he wished to declare himself Thekla's husband before this entity for which he had no name. That is what Thekla told me. I had not yet met Mr Solow. It was Bruno's idea to hold the ceremony in the cemetery chapel. It stood, unused for many years, near our country property in West Pomerania, in the middle of a garden-like cemetery behind a decaying palace, which had two birch trees growing symmetrically (how mysterious) from its crumbling facade, as if someone had placed them there instead of flags. An old travel guide claimed the chapel was built by a student of Schinkel's, though no one in the village knew anything about it. They had begun renovating the chapel five years ago, then stopped just as quickly as they had started. Since then a wide-open ladder stood under the blue cupola with silver stars, which always reminded me of the Count's favorite bow tie.

There were three steps at the front of the chapel leading to a gallery where a patch of artificial lawn, a hammer, and a broken statue of Christ, all on a stone base, joined to form a bizarre still life.

In the middle of the chapel there hung a tattered hemp rope ending in a noose. When I thoughtlessly pulled on it, the high-pitched passing bell rang. For days afterwards I was afraid I had provoked someone's death. But nothing happened, at least nothing I heard about. This forgotten temple of death, Bruno said, was a fitting place for Thekla Fleischer and Mr Solow's wedding. Though Bruno knew Mr Solow only from what I had told him, he seemed to have a great deal of sympathy for the older man. He even suggested that we, Bruno and I, arrange the wedding and he himself was prepared to perform the ceremony. Thekla was shocked at the thought of getting married in a house of the dead. She said it was blasphemy.

"Thekla," I said, "if God doesn't exist, he can't be offended. If He does exist, he'll understand and be glad there's so much love and imagination."

Mr Solow was enthusiastic. Since only death was stronger than his love for Thekla, he saw absolutely no reason why a death chapel was not a suitable venue for the vow he wished to take.

Thekla was still afraid, but she submitted to our euphoria.

When Mrs Wittig announced she was going to the Vogtland the coming weekend to visit an old schoolmate, Thekla and I bought a saddle of venison, wine, schnapps, and beer; Thekla packed snow-white, starched linen and one of her astonishing gowns - a grey, ankle-length satin smock with kimono sleeves. Saturday morning at eleven we picked Mr Solow up near his apartment and drove to the country.

There was snow on the fields and a white sun in the sky. "What a wonderful day, a real wedding day," Thekla exclaimed. Bruno started the furnace, while I put together a wedding bouquet in the garden from frozen rosebuds, ivy, rose hips, and pine branches. Thekla made the bed for herself and Mr Solow with the starched linen, trying to hide her embarrassment by behaving like a fussy housewife. Mr Solow looked on and told us how he had hiked through the Provence with a knapsack and twenty marks in his pocket the last summer before 1933; I thought, well, Mr Solow really is seventy, but he doesn't look his age. He was wearing jeans, a sailor's sweater with buttons on the shoulder, and a dark-red shawl, which he didn't take off once the house was warm.

Bruno larded the saddle of venison. Then we all changed clothes and drove to the next village, where the chapel was.

We took the narrow path between graves that looked as if the deceased had died only recently to a fire lane leading directly to the chapel along a small park - a unique avenue that was covered by a dense roof of trees during the summer, whose bare, intertwined branches reminded me of skeletons that had come together to play London Bridge with us.

Mr Solow held Thekla's left hand in his left, while his right hand was placed gently on her upper arm. He led her carefully over the steps covered with moss and small shrubs; Bruno stood at the end to receive the couple and accompany them into the chapel. I was the wedding procession.

Bruno delivered a short, very beautiful speech. He said that fate had brought Mr Solow and Thekla together along the path of life, to be sure a bit late, but they should recognize the justice they derived from this joy and the meaning this lent their previous misfortune. "For you, Thekla Fleischer, could not have recognized the beauty of Theodor Solow's soul if you had been after easy joy. And you, Theodor Solow, could not have recognized the beauty of this woman if your heart hadn't remained young and receptive to love."

Bruno said this. I couldn't believe my ears. Thekla wept.

Bruno had Mr Solow say I do, then Thekla. He then asked them to kneel to receive his blessing.

"And now the kiss," Bruno said.

The sky was black when we came out of the chapel. We were puzzled at where these huge dark clouds had come from all of a sudden.

"Oh God," Thekla said, "the sky is angry at

us."

"No," Mr Solow said, "it's simply showing its serious face."

A white lightning bolt tore the cloud cover apart and a few seconds later a roar of thunder shook the hallowed ground around us.

"They're playing the Beethoven Fifth in your honor," Bruno said.

Sharp freezing rain fell on us; we had a hard time getting back to our house along the slippery roads. Thekla's grey hair was filled with countless ice crystals; Mr Solow said that Thekla had to look quickly in the mirror to stop being afraid, because she would see that the storm was a wedding gift from heaven - a thousand gems for Thekla. Since bride's jewelry can be worn only once, it was all right for it to be transient. A minute later, Thekla's bride's jewelry ran like streams of tears over her face. It was like a day from another life. I didn't think of Beerenbaum for an instant.

That evening, as we were strolling through the village, I finally asked Thekla if she would teach me how to play the piano. We set the first lesson for the following week. Thekla and Mr Solow retired soon afterwards; Bruno and I were left alone and sat across from each other in the small room with the low ceiling as we used to before we were separated.

"Maybe we ought to get married, too," I said to Bruno.

"Later, Rosa," Bruno said. "We're still too young to be that grateful."

*

Since learning that Beerenbaum was responsible for the Count's arrest, I tried to imagine how I would ask him about it. I saw myself sitting at the small table with the typewriter, severe and upright. I would wait until it was so dark outside that Beerenbaum would have to turn on the table lamp and I could see his face. Then I would ask him: Do you know the Sinologist Karl-Heinz Baron? I would ask the question casually, as if I had just remembered the name and knew an amusing anecdote about the person in question. Or I would look Beerenbaum straight in the eye as Joan of Arc did with her inquisitor when she invoked her angel's commands, asking him in a clear, inflexible voice: Do you know the Sinologist Karl-Heinz Baron? Or I would open bluntly with the statement: You know the Sinologist Karl-Heinz Baron, don't you? in a mildly threatening tone of voice. Beerenbaum would deny ever having heard the name. He would try to use his guilty conscience as a pretext. After twenty years, he simply couldn't remember.

I left him no escape. You, Mr Beerenbaum, I would say very calmly, a working class lad from the Ruhr, professor with a primary school education, non-Latin with class instinct, Commissioner for Ideological Affairs at the University of Berlin at the time, sent a philologist of European rank to prison for three years because he mailed a parcel from the Potsdam Central Post Office.

Beerenbaum would be ashamed. Not because he had put the Count behind bars. He would have dismissed that as a political necessity, however unfortunate, as a marginal episode in the class struggle. He would feel shame at the realization that owing to his incomplete education, he was not entitled to do so.

I would take my coat and on my way to the door I would say, without so much as turning toward Beerenbaum: You were so afraid of education you had to imprison and expel it, solely out of fear.

This was how I imagined I would leave the defeated Beerenbaum.

I was too nervous to read or listen to the recording of *Don Giovanni* I had bought two weeks earlier. It was a mild day, so I decided to stroll through the park during the two hours I had left until my appointment with Beerenbaum. The park was a consoling welcome from another time. It had originally belonged to the palace to which Frederick the Great, whom Bruno simply called F Two, banished his wife once he could no longer tolerate her at court. A wide street led from Pankow church through the palace grounds to former Peace Square, now Ossietzky Square, in Niederschönhausen, something only old residents of Pankow knew. Since the palace had been proclaimed the seat of government in 1949, the street abruptly ended on both sides with a fence, completely barricaded on the Niederschönhausen side to the point of blocking the view of the palace, and on the Pankow side protected against unauthorized persons by heavily armed guards. To get from one part of the truncated street to the other, one had to take the tram five stops or go half an hour on foot. I had been living in this area for thirty years and had never mentally connected the two ends of the street. Not until Bruno, who found surveys and city maps as interesting as the real landscapes and residential areas they represent, effectively brought the Pankow streets closer together in my mind. Every time I had to submit our strolls to the arbitrary act of the palace occupiers, he cursed the insane rulers and desecrators of streets, who had not only closed off public walkways as they wished, but had also named an innocent square after the honorable Carl von Ossietzky to make everyone believe that Ossietzky had been a good friend of "our leader" Walter Ulbricht.

The park extended over a large area in such a way that it allowed a complete view of itself from all directions, making it possible at all times to make out acquaintances within it even if they were walking at the other end. Right now, around noon, it was almost empty. Two old women stood on the small arched bridge, throwing bread crumbs to the excited ducks that populated the Panke in both summer and winter. The Panke was a filthy, narrow river that flowed through the park from east to west and which lent its name to our city district. Three dogs frolicked on the field. Their owners, far from one another, waited patiently.

"You don't notice it so much from here" - the Count had exhaled this sentence like a sigh some time ago during a walk through the park. Since then we quoted him every time we discovered a halfway unspoiled oasis. You don't notice it so much from here. No explanation was required for what one didn't notice; the "so much" also meant not as bad as elsewhere. I've always wondered why they didn't do anything to the park - pour concrete over the paths, cut down the two- or three-hundred-year-old trees with their walled-off trunks. They hadn't even fenced it in like the palace or the "village." "Wherever we go the leaves wither," Anna Seghers is reported to have said. Miraculously, Seghers' "we" had spared the Pankow Palace Park. I looked for the first buds on the shrubs; they arched against the branches like tiny hard bellies.

I had been taking piano lessons from Thekla Fleischer for six weeks, every Wednesday from three to four. I stubbornly practised moving my two hands in various ways - a whole tone with the left, two halftones with the right: "Cuckoo, Cuckoo..." The piano literature wasn't organized for older pupils like me, Thekla said. For the time being, the vague longing that playing the piano was intended to satisfy was not fulfilled. Thekla, however, said that I had good motivation which would, to a certain extent, make up for my stiff joints. Every day I played scales for half an hour.

"Do you really think you'll be happier when you can play a little piece by Schubert?" Thekla asked.

"I won't be unhappier, that's for sure," I answered, and a woman over forty can't expect anything more than not growing unhappier.

"Yes," Thekla said. "Mama always used to comfort me with that when I was sad. 'Child, now you are dreaming of great success,' Mama would say, 'but in a few years you'll think you're happy if you haven't encountered a great misfortune.'"

For me, playing the piano, even if it was limited to scales and children's songs, was something like the park. You don't notice things so much while playing.

*

"Didn't the Comrade Major call you?" The housekeeper, dressed this time in a light-blue apron dress with white ruffles around the neck and shoulders, held on to the door handle, as though she would immediately close the door.

"Which Comrade Major?" I attempted to enter the house, but she shifted her pivot leg and closed the narrow crack between the door frame with her threatening hips.

"Young Mr Beerenbaum, of course, the Comrade Major. He must have phoned you to tell you not to come today."

I hadn't noticed before that she couldn't stand me. She stretched her short neck over the ruffles and stared at me angrily. "Herr Professor does not feel well, and that is why the

Comrade Major phoned you to tell you not to come today."

"He did not get in touch with me."

"Well," she raised her shoulders as if to say, too bad!

She obviously saw some connection between Beerenbaum's poor health and me. She was a faithful soul, and someone, probably Michael Beerenbaum, must have encouraged her to forbid me entry in this brusque, triumphant way. The end of her dustcloth hung out of her apron pocket. She smiled victorious, though I wasn't in the least aware I had been fighting against her too. That this Cerberus in a light-blue apron dress with white ruffles now refused me entry to a house which it took me a great effort to enter every time I came seemed to symbolize the tricky situation I had gotten myself into.

I was about to tell her that I hoped her Professor would soon be well, when Beerenbaum appeared behind her in a wool house coat. "But, Mrs Karl, please; if she's come, we want to ask her to come in."

She vacated the door, disappearing into the kitchen. Later, as she was serving the coffee, she smiled as she always did. "I'll bring the sugar on through to you right away." She had a peculiar talent for unnecessary prepositions.

Beerenbaum looked weak. The wrinkled skin of his face hung grey and superfluous on his chin bones. Even his hand shook more violently than usual, as if it had given up its final resistance. He slurped his coffee, barely able to lift his cup. Instead he let his weak, bent body sink forward a bit more until his mouth reached the edge of the cup. I suggested I come back another day, but he gestured no with his hand. "We are going to cover a pleasant chapter we won't have to fight over," he said. "Write: 'Return to Germany. The moment in which our train crossed the border into Germany was one of the happiest of my life. Home to liberated Germany, freed by the Soviet Army. All of the comrades in the train embraced and wept. In this hour we knew this would be our Germany, freed for all time from war-mongering imperialists and bloodthirsty fascists. We anticipated the difficult path, drenched in sweat and tears, that lay before us.'

"I would like to insert a poem here, he said, a poem by Johannes R. Becher,* which spoke to us from the heart with wonderful words."

He recited in his pathetic tone of voice:

> *You know how much it meant*
> *To walk the arduous road.*

---

*Johannes R. Becher was Minister of Culture of the East German state from 1954-58. [Ed.]

The path on all sides piled
With countless maimed and dead.
One thought alone, our vigor spent:
To rebuild our hallowed
Germany, though defiled.
The goal through all our dread.

Behold, the folk awaken!
To forge your life anew,
Despite the grueling way,
Rejoicing at your might.
Your steadfast faith unshaken.
Redoubled to pursue
Fresh tasks in freedom, yea
Ne'er again to quit your right!

The volume of air he could hold in his lungs was barely enough for the short verses; the last syllables were lost in his shortness of breath. He was that weak. Too weak for me to ask him about his guilt in the arrest and sentencing of the Count.

He dictated: "The minds of the people were in a terrible state ideologically. They were still closer to the murderers than to their victims. Anti-Soviet agitation had left deep traces in the working class as well. Educating these people was a task of gigantic dimensions."

He leaned back with his eyes closed. I observed him closely. Like people in the metro who fight an opponent silently to themselves - their boss, wife, or rival - while their face reflects the conversation, so now the memory of earlier victories passed across Beerenbaum's face. While I was following the complacent reminiscence in his changing expressions, I suddenly felt myself unintentionally imitating him - I lowered the corner of my mouth, raised my brows, wrinkled my forehead skeptically. And as an apparently necessary result of these masks, something within me imitated this expression, arousing a feeling any observer would have assumed I had within me. A hostile self-certainty sharpened my gaze at the frail Beerenbaum repeating his victories with relish. His arrogant contentment, heightened by his visible weakness, made my blood boil. Or the opposite - it was his weakness that disturbed me and aroused the memory of Beerenbaum's blood I had seen when I had tormented him with my questions about the Hotel Lux until it finally flowed out of his nose. He still kept his eyes shut, he was stretched out unprotected on his chair. I thought of his hyoid bone some- where between his chin and larynx. And then I asked: "Do you know the Sinologist Karl-Heinz Baron?"

He straightened himself up, smiled politely - he hadn't understood anything, nothing had happened. But I asked again: "Do you know the Sinologist Karl-Heinz Baron?"

He answered, without hesitating, although he drew out the words as if to gain time - Yes, he knew him, although that was a long time ago.

"Do you remember your last meeting with him?"

"There were only two. I remember both of them." He raised his hand, like a speaker, to ask for silence, a gesture from his past when he still sat in front of conference tables, yielding or denying the floor. "Did you get the last sentence?" he asked. "'Educating these people was a task of gigantic dimensions.'"

I imagined he had condemned the Count to silence with this hand gesture, while the Count nervously, clumsily tried to invent a non-punishable connection between the escaped traitor, himself, and the parcel he had mailed to West Berlin from the Potsdam Central Post Office.

It isn't because I do not know what happened that I find the following events hard to remember. I know these minutes exactly as if I had lived through them twofold, as a spectator and as an actor. Actually, I was present in a threefold capacity, because I was also divided as an actor - into one who did something and another who wished to do something. I know everything; nothing escaped me. That is what makes it so hard to remember.

I see them in front of me: Beerenbaum and Rosalind. He is sitting behind the desk caught in the yellow light of the table lamp. She is sitting opposite him, two paces away, entrenched behind the Rheinmetall typewriter.

While I was still undecided whether justice demanded revenge for the Count or consideration for the ailing Beerenbaum, Rosalind had already made up her mind. The tiny hairs standing on end on her forearm as well as her concentrated gaze, impervious to signals demanding pity, announced her attack. I saw it, and Beerenbaum saw it too.

She ignored his last attempt to block dialogue: "Please, Rosa, another time, not today." I don't know why he didn't simply get up and leave the room. Perhaps he lacked the strength to do even that.

Rosalind interrogated him. "Where did you get the right? Were you convinced of his guilt?" She began calmly, then sat enthroned like an avenging goddess behind the typewriter. Beerenbaum had surrendered. One could now believe he was giving in to something he had long expected. "I myself was persecuted," he said, his voice almost toneless. "Grete was in a concentration camp. It is not an easy matter to send a man to jail. We're not monsters. Communists fought against monsters. We weren't permitted to go to university. We paid so that others could go to university, always. First, as proletarians with our sweat, then with the money of our state. The Workers' Penny. This education was our property; anyone who ran away with it was a robber, your Sinologist was a thief, yes, indeed. A thief belongs in prison."

Rosalind bent forward, her arms resting on the typewriter keys. With every syllable she jerked her head in the air like a barking dog. "Confiscating brains. You confiscated grey matter because you had too little of it yourselves. In the century to come you would have amputated them and hung them on wires to save prison costs. Servitude of the mind instead of serfdom of the body. You liberators of mankind had enough body, but you lacked brains. Do you know Latin? You do not know Latin, therefore you forbade others to learn Latin. Those who did were thrown in jail so everyone would forget such a thing as Latin existed. Everything had to be forgotten in order that people didn't find out anything you didn't know."

Supported by his healthy hand, Beerenbaum

tried again to sit up straight in his chair. His voice was compressed, breathless with pain or rage: "We have forgotten nothing. Never. We always knew what hunger and cold were, damp apartments, rickets, unemployment, war. Our university was class struggle. Our Latin was Marx and Lenin. Go forward and do not forget. You have forgotten. What do you really know?"

"Nothing. We know nothing," Rosalind cried, her face so twisted she could barely recognize herself. "Nothing, because we were not allowed to live. Your own life was not enough for you, it was too mean, so you used up our life, too. You are cannibals, slave owners with an army of torturers."

I heard Rosalind screeching, I saw her spray her saliva and bang her fists on the typewriter. The worst thing - it was reflected in her eyes - she did not actually do was this: Rosalind standing in front of Beerenbaum, her fists raised to strike, her other hand on Beerenbaum's neck between chin and larynx. Her fist hits his face. His dentures fall out of his mouth. She continues hitting him until he falls from his chair. The wool house coat opens above his legs and Beerenbaum's withered thighs lie naked on the floor, his soft genitals visible underneath his white underwear. She kicks his ribs, his head, his testicles; she jumps on his rib cage with both legs. He does not stir. When she sees blood coming out of his ear, she gives up, exhausted.

Beerenbaum leaned back in the chair behind the desk. The only part of him still alive was his hand condemned to endless shaking. "You *are* my enemy," he whispered.

Although she had stopped talking, there was still something ominous in the air between them. Only Rosalind seemed to know what would happen. She stared at the defeated Beerenbaum as in a trance. He slowly raised his head; I then saw from his face that he was frightened to death. He drew air through his half-open mouth with a gasp. His healthy hand clenched his chest where his breathing expired in a rattle. The other hand grasped at nothingness, looking for support. Rosalind saw the hand stretched out toward her, saw the dying Beerenbaum, and waited for his death. When I finally understood she would not do anything to save him, I got back my voice.

The housekeeper knew where to find the box with the Nitrangin capsules. I called the emergency doctor. Beerenbaum was taken to the hospital. I saw him only once after that.

*

It kills me that I can be so happy when other people die. For the second time in my life I am walking behind a coffin and am taking leave of someone without mourning. In F. a thirty-two-year-old unskilled laborer strangled his fiancée because she wanted to leave him. He couldn't bear the thought of her continuing to live without loving him. He deleted her lack of love like a computer error by "erasing" the woman. I looked for Beerenbaum's hyoid bone only with my eyes. I did not place my hands around his neck and squeeze my thumb against his throat. I didn't do that. But like the unskilled laborer from F., I too could only think of one way out: Beerenbaum's death. Why didn't the unskilled laborer from F. look for another woman to forget the injury that had been done to him? What kept him chained to his fiancée, who no longer wished to have him in her life? Why didn't I go my own way, learn to play the piano with Thekla Fleischer, finally begin to translate the recitatives to *Don Giovanni*? Why did I not submit to the answer I long suspected to Toller's question: Yes, the agent must undergo guilt, again and again; or if he does not wish to undergo guilt, perish. It was as if I had sought only my own guilt. Anything to avoid being a victim. Herbert Beerenbaum, the worker from the Ruhr, knew that as well:

Anything to avoid once again becoming a victim.

Only now do I recognize the housekeeper in the next to last row. Her fleshy thighs rise and fall beneath her tight black coat. Her wobbly gait and her thin, sinewy legs (at least in proportion to her bulky body) make her look like a camel. She holds in her chafed hands a small bouquet of red carnations and a handkerchief with which she occasionally wipes her eyes. Mrs Karl is one of those people who consider themselves to be unimportant: "I'm really not important." Mrs Karl has used her unimportance to serve the Professor, whom she considers important. I surmised Mrs Karl would think nothing of being a victim. That sets her apart from Beerenbaum and me. There have to be the common people too, she says, and work ennobles. Mrs Karl had once worked for a few years as matron in a women's prison. "It wasn't always pleasant," she said, once when I was waiting for Beerenbaum in the kitchen.

As she held the panting Beerenbaum by the hand, she kept trying to encourage him, saying, "Stay calm, the doctor will be here in a minute, keep very calm." She gave me, her master's murderer, several hate-filled glances. "I told you you shouldn't have come today," she hissed when Beerenbaum was pushed into the ambulance on a stretcher. "Now why don't you just go, so the Comrade Major won't have to find you here." Then she ran into the house, whimpering.

I felt sick, my forehead was hot, and my teeth clattered. I went to bed. No sooner had I closed my eyes than I saw Beerenbaum, half dead, stretching out his hand toward me. He bared his teeth as my father did when he cleaned the crumbs from his dentures with his tongue. I folded my hands under the sheets and prayed for him not to die, for me not to have killed him. I prayed as I had prayed as a child when the children next door secretly took me to Sunday school: "Dear God, don't..."

I shouldn't have asked him. Shouldn't I have asked him? He was seventy-eight years old. He had heart disease.

When he was fifty-five and healthy, he had handed the Count over to the Security Police. At the time no one would have dared to ask what right he had to lock up other people. And now he barricaded himself behind his weakness. My teeth chattered furiously. Dear God, don't make him die. I shouldn't have hated him like that.

That evening Thekla came and brewed fennel tea with thyme syrup. "Mama always used to make it when I had a fever - fennel tea with thyme syrup and wet compresses around the lower legs," she said, wrapping my legs in wet towels.

"I'm to blame if he dies," I said.

"Nonsense," Thekla said. She wrapped me in the blanket like a mummy. "You've got to sweat now. If someone does things in his life," she said and plopped heavily on the foot of my bed, "if someone does such terrible things, if you ask me, it's his own fault if he dies." She pulled her feet up on the bed and leaned back far enough so that when she looked through the upper part of the window, she could see the second floor of the house opposite, where Mr Solow's daughter lived.

"Tell me something about him," I said.

"Really?" Thekla exclaimed and clapped her hands. They had met only yesterday at eleven in front of the Pergamon Altar, almost accidentally. They walked around all the magnificent objects there as in a lost world. Later, Mr Solow took her to dinner at the Moscow Restaurant. Thekla said she was sure he could never have done anything as horrible as Beerenbaum.

"Yes," I said, "but I met Beerenbaum and you met Mr Solow. I'm afraid it was more than chance."

Thekla stayed until I fell asleep.

*

The pallbearers carefully let the coffin slide across belts into the grave. Michael Beerenbaum, his wife, his son, and the double chin are standing next to one another, six or seven feet from the grave. Later, when it's my turn to throw three handfuls of earth on Beerenbaum's coffin, I will have to approach them. I will extend my hand, afraid that no one will take it, and have to say: My heartfelt condolences. I am still hidden behind the black backs of the others, who walk up to the grave one by one, where an employee of the cemetery has made sure that there is enough room between the wreathes and bouquets for a pair of feet. Each of them reaches three times into a metal container and throws moist sand into the grave. Ashes to ashes, dust to dust. The sand falls on the wooden coffin lid with a dull sound. This is the sound I came to hear.

The housekeeper lets her bouquet of carnations fall into the hole in the ground. She feebly raises her coarse arm, hesitantly opens her hand, fingers slightly bent, which she holds in the air for a moment as a final farewell to her master - an elegiac gesture she must have seen in the movies. She sobs into her handkerchief as she throws the sand. I can't tell whether she is mourning sincerely or whether she believes she owes him this proof of grieving. She shakes Michael Beerenbaum's hand in sympathy, shakes that of his wife rather briefly and embraces the boy. Five more black backs in front of me. I'm last again. The housekeeper remains at a seemly distance from the family. Now she recognizes me. I can tell what she will say later about this moment: "I thought I was going to die."

The freesia fall between the coffin and the freshly dug walls of the grave. Under the carved coffin lid between the silk cushions is Beerenbaum in his dove-grey suit. I refuse to think of Beerenbaum's hand. It is over. I reach into the cold sand. Let him cast the first stone... I let the sand run slowly through my fingers onto the coffin. It is over. When I turn around I am standing opposite all of them and they train their eyes on me. Michael Beerenbaum's eyes with their dull, glassy sheen are also looking at me. Before I can take the three steps to them and put out my hand, he turns away. I am relieved. I put my hand into my coat pocket, throw the balls of newspaper onto a pile of old grave ornaments behind a boxwood shrub. The mourners move toward the main entrance in small groups. Only the housekeeper is walking alone. I keep my distance. The housekeeper bends down, tightens her shoelaces until she sees my feet next to hers, straightens up, and spits into the sand with pursed lips. "You shameless creature," she says. She must have gotten that from a film, too. Then she quickly catches up with the others.

I walk slowly, leaving enough space between the black backs and myself so that I can hear my own footsteps again. It is still cold. The sky hangs motionless and grey over the graves like a charred ceiling. Nothing happens. Why doesn't this damn sky open up and disgorge a flood or a burst of sunshine that can start blazes or at least a medium storm like the one after Thekla's wedding. Beerenbaum is dead and buried. And it is as if everything were over. The day after tomorrow is the day after Beerenbaum's death.

When is the day after tomorrow? Tomorrow, the day before yesterday, the day after tomorrow? Did the day after tomorrow pass by already without my noticing it?

When I was twenty-one, I traveled abroad for the first time. I stood in the evening sun on the Charles Bridge in Prague, waiting for something tremendous to happen, for something I could not have experienced if I hadn't been here. But I couldn't make out anything. I was delighted to hear a foreign language I couldn't understand. I looked at Malá Strana with its narrow, intact lanes, and all I could feel was endless disappointment. My soul, or so it seemed, was too small to permit the miracle I was waiting for, and I thought things would stay like this for all time, that I would never experience what I longed for so long as I was present. I spat into the Vltava and walked up to Hradcany Castle. Much later I discovered in my memory these minutes on the Charles Bridge and the view from the Castle over the roofs of Prague, which radiated a golden glow in the late afternoon sun as intense as everyone says. But most of all I remembered the irritating feeling of not belonging, the beautiful intoxication of being foreign. I felt like the brothers who by order of their dying father had dug up an entire vineyard in search of a buried treasure, and when they had found neither gold nor jewels, criticized the futility of their efforts and, probably, the meanness of their father. The following summer, though - the brothers had learned to live with their disappointment - the prophesied treasure was there as an overly abundant harvest on the vines.

By now the others have walked through the grey stone gate and turned on to the street. I wait until the bus has passed the cemetery exit in the direction of the city, and I am certain that I will not find one of Beerenbaum's mourners at the bus stop, before I start walking faster. When I get home I'll drink tea, maybe listen to *Don Giovanni*, and, later, once my hands are warm again, I'll practise scales.

As I reach the street, I see Michael Beerenbaum's crimson-red car in the parking lot; he is just opening the car door and getting out. He comes toward me. Wearing his uniform he has the face of a military man, not a pastor or pathologist. His gait is also different, soldierly. He is holding a parcel wrapped in newspaper in his hands. "Here," he says, when he is standing in front of me. "He wanted you to have this." His voice does not betray whether he approves of his father's wish. I know what is in the parcel. I do not want it. I no longer want to have anything to do with it. Nonetheless, I take it.

I am still standing in front of the cemetery as the crimson-red car disappears beyond the curve, with the thin parcel in my hand wrapped in yesterday's paper like a pound of herring. I shall not open it. I shall throw it in the next rubbish bin. I shall bury it between the mountains of paper on the lowest shelf of my bookcase. Under no circumstances shall I open it.

* * *

About the translator: David Newton Marinelli translated Monika Maron's two previous novels, *Flight of Ashes* (Readers International, 1986) and *The Defector* (Readers International, 1988). Mr Marinelli has also translated works by Thomas Bernhard, Hermann Kant and Guido Gozzano. His recently published translations include *Magic Prague* by Angelo Maria Ripellino (Macmillan and University of California Press), *Musical Life in a Changing Society* by Kurt Blaukopf (Amadeus Press), and the forthcoming *Antonio Vivaldi* by Karl Heller (Amadeus Press). He obtained a Bachelor of Arts degree in history at Ohio State University and two Masters of Arts and a Doctor of Philosophy degree at Rutgers University (New Jersey, USA). After working for twelve years in Vienna, he recently returned to live in the United States, where he is working on a biography of the Czech composer Josef Suk.